Sadie Rose
AND THE DARING ESCAPE

A PRAIRIE YOUTH ADVENTURE

Sadie Rose
AND THE
DARING ESCAPE

Hilda Stahl

CROSSWAY BOOKS • WESTCHESTER, ILLINOIS
A DIVISION OF GOOD NEWS PUBLISHERS

Dedicated with love
to Brad and Dawn Stahl

Special thanks to
Mable Proctor
Belva Lowery
Joanne Hesselink
Jay Clements
Zelma Clements

Sadie Rose and the Daring Escape. Copyright © 1988 by Hilda Stahl. Published by Crossway Books, a division of Good News Publishers, Westchester, Illinois 60153.

Cover illlustration by Kathy Kulin.

Book design by K. L. Mulder.

Second printing, 1989

Printed in the United States of America

Library of Congress Catalog Card Number 88-70496

ISBN 0-89107-492-9

Contents

1

Jake's Crossing

Sadie touched her hot face and licked her dry lips. The late afternoon sun blazed down and took away the coolness inside the covered wagon. When would York stop so she could get a drink?

Bossie bawled, and Sadie knew Bossie would have to be milked the minute they reached York's place. She and Web usually took turns, but during the trip Momma and Opal milked also. Sadie couldn't remember whose turn it was today. She glanced out at Riley, drooping in the saddle on the big bay.

She tried to block out the laughter from Opal playing cat's cradle with Helen and Web.

York turned on the seat and poked his head in the opening of the wagon. "Jake's Crossing up ahead, kids. We'll get supplies and in another hour be home."

The others shouted happily, but Sadie sat as if she hadn't heard. She wanted to clamp her hands over her ears, but she didn't dare. She closed her eyes and watched the Sadie she saw behind her eyelids. That Sadie had her hands clamped over her ears and her tongue stuck way out at York. That Sadie was an ornery girl, a fussy baby—and not at all a grown-up twelve-year-old. "And I don't care," she announced under her breath.

"Put your shoes on, children," said Momma quietly. "And make yourselves presentable."

Sadie opened her eyes, tugged on her shoes, tied them, then looked out over Web's head.

More dust rose up behind the wagon now because they were on a road rather than the grassy prairie. Sand spit out from the back wheels. They passed a small house made of new wood. A woman with a baby in her arms stood in front, her hand shielding the sun from her eyes as she watched them.

Web waved, and the woman waved back and smiled slightly.

Helen crowded between Web and Sadie. "Who'd you wave to, Web?"

"Her."

"Oh." Helen waved, but the woman had turned back into the house and didn't see. Helen waited until they passed another house, saw two boys playing in the yard, and waved to them. They waved back, and she smiled proudly.

"Let *me* see," said Opal, straining to see out. "Did you see any fine young men?"

Sadie groaned. "Do little boys count?"

"There's one!" cried Helen, pointing at a man riding a sorrel. He lifted his hat, and Opal jerked back with a little squeal.

Sadie laughed. "There's another one, Opal."

Opal frowned. "That's Riley. Brothers don't count."

"Riley, can I ride again?" shouted Web.

"Children . . ." said Momma, clicking her tongue.

Sadie knew that meant not to raise your voice in town and to mind your manners.

Riley rode up close and reached for Web. Opal steadied him on the back of the wagon, and Riley lifted him easily into the saddle with him.

Sadie watched as they passed two more houses, then a church with a livery across from it.

York pulled the team to a stop at the water trough in front of two more homes. Not a tree was in sight—only the prairie grasses waving in the wind and the hot sun shining down from the giant bright blue sky.

York helped Momma down and kept hold of her longer than necessary. She looked up at him and smiled, and Sadie looked quickly away so she wouldn't see the light in Momma's brown eyes.

"Girls, you can come with me or wait here," said Momma. She was a head shorter than York, and rounded where he was lean. Her brown and yellow calico dress covered her shoes and touched the dusty ground. Her matching sunbonnet covered dark hair that Sadie knew had strands of gray in it.

"I'm comin'," said Opal, smoothing her hair, tying her bonnet neatly in place and smoothing her dress before she reached down for York to lift her to the ground.

"Me too," said Helen, flinging herself into York's strong arms.

"I'll wait here," said Sadie stiffly.

York smiled at her and she forced a small smile,

but her stomach knotted painfully. She couldn't let herself care for York or she'd be disloyal to Pa. York settled his wide-brimmed hat in place and strode over to Momma and Opal with Helen still in his arms. He glanced at Riley as he rode up. "Riley, water Bossie right away."

Sadie looked away to watch Riley stop the bay beside a mule and drop the reins over the rail. He watered Bossie with Web's help, then walked with Web after York. Riley looked different with the wide-brimmed hat shielding his handsome face.

The wind brought smells of the horses, but also an occasional whiff of bread baking.

An old bearded man stood in the doorway of the general store and didn't move until York asked him to. With a lurch he leaned against the sod storefront, his battered hat low over his eyes.

Sadie turned away just in time to see a movement near the mule's front hooves.

"A dog," she muttered. It lifted its head for a moment and let it fall again. It was a dirty brown with small, pointed ears. She hadn't noticed it when Riley dismounted.

Pa had always had a dog that went with him everywhere he went. He missed Pa and wouldn't eat for a long time after Pa was gone. They had to leave Racer behind because he was too old to make the trip.

Sadie touched her flat stomach. She hadn't eaten much either, until Momma had forced her to.

Somehow she had to convince Momma to let her go back to live with Emma so she could be near Pa's grave. But if she did that, she couldn't help take care of the family. She remembered York and his position as pa now, and her eyes clouded over. "They don't need me," she whispered.

Again she felt thirsty, so she climbed down and filled the dipper from the water in the barrel on the side of the wagon. The water was warm, but wet her lips and satisfied her thirst.

The team shook the harness and moved restlessly. From the livery a horse whinnied.

Just then the old man, his salt-and-pepper beard touching his belt, staggered to the mule. He tipped his battered hat—as dirty as his ragged shirt and pants—to Sadie, and she slightly inclined her head. She glanced at his feet to see boots that shone as bright as Momma's copper boiler after she'd polished it. Suddenly he lifted a boot and kicked the dog. The dog let out a startled yap.

"Hey!" cried Sadie, jumping forward.

The man kicked the dog again.

It yelped and tried to stand, but fell as the man kicked it again.

"Get up, you lazy, no-good pup."

Sadie could see the dog's ribs and as the man raised his shiny boot to kick again, she leaped forward, sending puffs of dust onto her shoes and legs. "Don't kick that dog!"

The man looked up in surprise. "What's that ya say?"

"Don't kick that dog!" Sadie stood over the pup, her eyes blazing and bright circles of red in her cheeks. "Don't!"

"I can kick the pup if I want, little girl. What's to stop me?"

"I'll stop you!" She stood bravely over the dog with her thin shoulders square and her chin high.

"Ain't you the feisty little prairie chicken." The man chuckled and shook his head, his salt-and-pepper beard swinging back and forth. "That pup ain't worth his keep. I don't know why I bothered with him this long. I'd as leave shoot him as look at him."

"No! Don't!"

"It's my dog and I can do what I dad blame please." He reached for the long rifle in the boot of his saddle.

Sadie cried out and rammed against him, sending him sprawling to the ground. His hat flew off, showing a balding pink head. She doubled her fists and stood with her feet apart, her dark eyes narrowing into slits. "You can't shoot that dog!"

The man swore, clamped his hat back on, and jumped up. He drew back his fist and slugged, but Sadie leaped out of his way and the blow fell short.

"He's gonna die, prairie chicken." Once again the man grabbed for his rifle, but once again Sadie rammed against him. He caught himself before he fell, and his face darkened with fresh anger. He lunged for her, brushed against her, and sent them both sprawling side by side to the dust. He wrapped a strong arm around her before she could roll clear of him. She choked as she kicked her legs and thrashed her arms, trying to break free. The smell of his sweat and tobacco turned her stomach.

Suddenly the man was lifted away from her, and she looked up to see a tall, muscular man with sweat-stained blue shirt, heavy pants, and dust-covered boots hold the small man in the air.

As she watched, a boy about Riley's age helped her to her feet. He was tall and lean and dressed the way York had dressed Riley. "Are you all right?" he asked gently.

She shook sand off her dress, nodded, and glanced back at the two men.

"What's goin' on, Ty Bailer?" asked Sadie's rescuer in a pleasant voice that didn't match the look on his sun-darkened face.

"None of yer business, Joshua Cass!" Ty Bailer squirmed, but couldn't get away. "Put me down!"

"Not yet. Suppose you tell me what the fight was all about."

"She attacked me," said Ty.

Joshua Cass nodded. "I could see it was an equal fight."

"He kicked the dog and he was going to kill it," said Sadie in a low, tight voice.

The boy moved closer to her, and she felt safer.

Joshua Cass nodded and dropped Ty Bailer to the ground, but kept hold of his upper arm. "Dogs and kids—girls at that, Ty. How low will you go? Try kickin' babies next?"

Ty scowled and worked at the strong fingers gripping his arm. "That dog's no good. It's half-starved same as me, and it's too dumb to train."

"You can't kill him!" said Sadie sharply.

"He won't," said Joshua Cass. "Hear that, Ty?"

Ty nodded, and finally Joshua let him go. The old man reached for the reins, then untied the dog from the post and yanked the rope until the dog half-hung in the air.

Sadie's heart stopped.

"You're not takin' the dog," said Joshua Cass. He held out his large hand, and finally Ty dropped the rope in it.

Sadie's face lit up, and she glanced at the boy beside her.

He smiled and nodded.

Ty glared at Sadie. "You can take my pup if

13

you're so inclined, but I'll get it back and you'll be a sorry little prairie chicken. A plucked, sorry prairie chicken."

Sadie shivered.

"Don't harm the girl," said Joshua Cass in a hard voice, "or you'll have me to answer to."

Sadie watched Ty Bailer mount his mule and ride away in a small cloud of dust. Finally she looked down at the big glazed eyes of the mongrel pup.

"Now what?" asked Joshua Cass.

Sadie knelt beside the dog and touched its thin side and stroked its large head. "You're comin' with me, pup." She looked up at the man and boy. "I'll take care of him."

Joshua nodded and grinned. "And just who are you?"

"Sadie . . . York."

"York?"

"My momma and York got married, and we're movin' in with him."

"You don't say!" Joshua slapped his thigh with his hat, sending dust flying as he laughed. "You don't say!" He clamped his hand on the boy's shoulder. "This is my boy Levi, and I'm Joshua Cass. We have a place west of here."

The name Levi struck her, and she couldn't speak for a minute. Pa's name was Levi.

"You put up quite a fight before we could get to you," said Levi, grinning.

"I couldn't let him hurt the dog."

Levi knelt beside the pup. "He looks bad, Paw."

Joshua crouched next to the dog and gently ran his big hands over him.

"He doesn't deserve a dog," whispered Sadie savagely.

14

"He starves Tanner," said Levi.

"That's his name?"

"I call him that. Old Ty don't call him nothin'."

"He's in a bad way, but with care he'll make it," said Joshua.

"I'm takin' him with me." Then she thought of York, and she shivered. York might object to a strange, half-dead dog living at his place.

The pup whined.

"I'll take you with me no matter what!" Gently, awkwardly she lifted the pup in her arms. But before she could move, Levi took the pup from her.

"Tell me where to put him."

"In the wagon." She scrambled in and moved aside a box that held Momma's seeds.

Gently Levi laid Tanner in place. He patted Tanner's head and smiled at Sadie. "You sure put up a good fight."

A shaft of pleasure pierced Sadie's heart. "Thanks. But if your pa hadn't helped me . . ." Her voice died away.

"My pleasure," said Joshua. He squeezed Sadie's shoulder. "I hope to see you again, Sadie York." He turned to Levi. "Meet me at the livery in a few minutes."

Levi nodded before he reached in and stroked Tanner again. "I'm glad Ty Bailer don't have Tanner no more. I'm glad you fought for him. I wanted to the two times I saw him beat Tanner, but I knew Ty would kill me if I tried."

Sadie's dark eyes grew big and round. "Will he really try to kill me?"

Levi moved restlessly and finally nodded. "He might. But York'll protect you. And Paw will if he can." He looked down at Tanner. "So will I."

Sadie's heart fluttered. "Thanks."

"Tanner's not much to look at, but he's a good pup. He'll make a fine dog when he's full growed." Levi stepped away from the wagon. "I hope to see you again too, Sadie York."

She nodded and smiled slightly before he turned and strode toward the sod livery. She watched until he disappeared inside.

Tanner whined, tried to lift his head, but couldn't.

Sadie touched a pointed ear. "I'll take good care of you, boy. I promise. I won't let you die." She dug out a quilt that she'd helped stitch and covered him carefully. "You be quiet, Tanner. I don't know if York'll want me to keep you. But I'm goin' to anyway. I'm goin' to take good care of you, and that's a promise."

2

Remembering

Sadie blinked back tears and tried to force down the terrible lump in her throat. "I don't want to move all the way to the edge of the sandhills," she whispered weakly. She leaned against the end-gate of the covered wagon and watched the spring prairie grasses rippling in the constant Nebraska wind. She felt all alone even with Opal, Web, and Helen in the wagon with her and Momma and York on the seat and Riley out somewhere riding in the hills around them. Having Tanner hidden beside her eased the pain just slightly.

Sadie scowled and leaned her head on her arms, resting on the end-gate. Since they'd left Jake's Crossing she'd seen nothing but grass and birds and prairie dogs and, of course, tied securely to the wagon, Bossie, their milk cow that Momma had wanted brought along from Douglas County.

Suddenly a hawk swooped down from the sky,

barely touched the top of the grass, and rose again with a rabbit gripped in its talons.

Sadie gasped and leaned forward. Life had been snatched from the rabbit just as it had been from Pa last winter when he'd frozen in the blizzard.

A tear dripped from Sadie's pale cheek onto her clenched hand. Pictures of Pa struggling through the howling wind and a swirling mass of snow flashed through her mind. How terrible it would be to fight against the cold wind and snow only to lose in the end.

She trembled and almost cried out in anguish. Pa had thought she was walking home from Emma's, and he'd walked to meet her so she wouldn't get lost. Somehow in the wind and the snow he'd lost his way, and without shelter he had frozen to death.

Sadie clamped her hand over her mouth to hold back the sobs. All the time Pa had been fighting the blizzard, she'd been laughing and talking to Emma, safe and snug at Emma's house while the wind howled and the snow whipped up into drifts higher than a horse's back.

"Oh, Pa," she whispered into her hand. When she'd learned that Pa had frozen to death, she'd frozen inside and she'd promised herself that as long as she lived she'd be good and she'd spend her life watching out for Momma and the kids and she'd never marry. That had been her solemn vow. She'd kept it month after month, taking over many of the chores with Riley that Pa would've done, talking to Momma about their future plans for the farm, and helping with the kids without being mean or raising her voice at them.

And then York had come along, and Momma had married him without so much as asking how she felt! York. He'd been an orphan, and the man who had found him, kicking and crying under a cactus, had named him York after his old home in England. York said he'd been hatched under that cactus. Web had said that he must've been tiny to hatch under a cactus, but York laughed and said, "A cactus in Texas is bigger than the baby ones in Nebraska. A whole family could live in the shade of a Texas prickly pear." They'd all laughed except Sadie, and she'd wanted to tell him she knew he was lying. Grown-ups didn't call it lying. They called it telling tall tales. All of them, especially Momma, thought York was wonderful.

Sadie bit her bottom lip and tasted sand. Momma hadn't listened at all when she'd begged her not to marry York, or when she begged her not to sell the homestead, or when she begged her not to move away.

Sadie forced back a moan that had started deep down inside her.

Who would take care of Pa's grave now?

Emma White had promised that she would, but Sadie knew Emma would get busy with other things and forget.

Sadie twisted her sunbonnet string. How could she keep the promise of taking care of the family now that it was York's job?

"What're you lookin' at, Sadie?" asked Opal from the crate on which she sat stitching.

"Nothin'."

"Let's talk."

"No."

"I want to talk." Opal's voice was soft as the feather tick that covered nine-year-old Web and eight-year-old Helen as they slept. They'd tried to stay awake after Jake's Crossing, but had finally given in. "Let's talk about fallin' in love."

"No!"

"About havin' our own babies."

"No!"

"Are you still pouting because you didn't want to move?"

"Leave me alone!"

Opal gripped the hoop that held her stitching taut. "We always used to talk about how it would be to fall in love and get married and have our own place and babies of our own."

"Talk to yourself." Sadie knew she should be polite, but right now she couldn't.

"Sadie?"

"Leave me alone!"

"I'm fourteen and you're twelve and I can make you do what I say," snapped Opal.

Sadie turned toward her sister with a scowl. Opal sat with her stitching forgotten on her lap. Her blue calico dress hugged her comfortably and covered her knees and almost touched the tops of her bare feet. Her sunbonnet hung down her back with her long brown braids. Her blue eyes flashed with anger, but Sadie didn't care. She knew her brown eyes were just as full of anger. "No, you can't make me talk if I don't want to!"

"Yes, I can!"

"You can't!"

"You make me so mad!"

Sadie turned away. "I just don't want to talk right now, Opal. I don't want to wake up Web and Helen." Sadie knew it was a lie and she flushed, but didn't take it back. She had never told lies in the past, nobody in the family did, but now she was different.

"Those two kids won't wake up by hearin' us talk, and you know it. You're bein' mean." Opal was silent a while. "I just won't talk to you either! I'll pretend you're not even here. Momma should've let you stay in Douglas County!"

Sadie locked her hands over the end-gate and watched their wagon tracks stretch behind them until the two lines seemed to run together and disappear. Bright blue sky bigger than the land dipped down, down to the ground to touch green waving grasses. Warm spring wind gusted against her, almost blowing her hair loose from the tight braids, and she moved back just enough to be out of it. Smells of leather and canvas and springtime stirred up by the wind filled her nostrils. The rattle of the harness, the flap of the white canvas, and the creak of the wagon broke the great silence of the vast prairie.

Sadie swallowed hard to force back the lump in her throat. For a minute tears blurred her vision, but she blinked them away before Opal saw them. Opal wouldn't understand tears. She was happy about traveling across Nebraska to the rim of the sandhills.

Opal had said she'd find a fine young man to marry so she could have a place of her own. She'd said all the land was taken in the eastern part of the state. She'd said all the fine young men were taken too. But what she really meant was that Randall Ervin had up and married Nora Greenwood without telling a soul. Opal had planned to marry Randall once she'd turned sixteen. But Randall hadn't waited, him already being eighteen.

Sadie carefully brushed away her tears and peeked back at Opal, but she was engrossed in her stitching.

Didn't Opal still hurt over Pa's death? But then, Opal hadn't been to blame for it.

Sadie stared out the back of the wagon just as a

jackrabbit stood tall, its ears almost as long as its body, then bounded away out of sight behind a grassy knoll.

She heard York's deep voice and Momma's laugh, and her stomach tightened into an icy ball. How could Momma laugh with him? How could she move two hundred miles west with him and leave behind her old life?

And Pa's grave.

Sadie picked at a patch that she'd sewed over a hole in her dress. She knew that only Pa's body was in the grave and that he had gone to Heaven to live with Jesus. She understood all that, but it hadn't helped. She had been able to touch the grave and keep it clear of weeds and brighten it up with flowers when possible. Now both the grave where his body lay and Heaven where his spirit lived were beyond her touch.

Suddenly she flipped around and glared at Opal. "Don't you ever get tired of stitching?" Even as the words sprang forward she wanted to grab them back.

Opal looked up with a frown. "What's wrong with you, Sadie?"

Sadie smoothed her faded dress over her thin legs, looked down at her bare feet, then stared right at Opal. "I want to know why you sit and stitch that dumb sampler all the time."

Opal narrowed her blue eyes that looked so much like Pa's that Sadie felt fresh tears sting her eyes. "I never know what mood you're going to be in, Sadie Rose Merrill. I mean, Sadie Rose York."

Sadie cringed at the sound of the new name Momma had insisted they take when she married York. She'd said, "A new name and a new start. Yesterday's behind us and tomorrow waits for us. Today we're going to be happy."

"York is a nice name, but I liked Merrill, too."

Opal touched her rosy cheek and brushed back a strand of wavy, nutmeg-brown hair that had escaped the braid. "Of course, I will have a new name again once I turn sixteen and get married."

Sadie hugged her thin body. "You just might be an old maid, you know."

Opal's eyes flashed. "Don't you dare say that to me!"

"Old maid!" Sadie felt mean, but she couldn't stop her tongue. "Old maid Opal Margaret Merrill York!"

Color drained from Opal's face and she jabbed her needle at Sadie, barely pricking the bare part of her leg below her dress. "You take that back right now!"

"I won't!" Sadie watched the growing dot of bright red blood on her leg, then leaned forward and spat out, "I won't!"

"Girls, girls." Momma twisted around, leaned into the wagon, and clicked her tongue. Her bonnet brushed the canvas of the wagon, and her face was in shadows.

Sadie clamped her mouth closed, and Opal picked up her stitching and bent over it once again. Sadie wanted to say more to Opal, but she knew Momma wouldn't allow it. Finally Momma turned around and said something to York.

"You're mean," whispered Opal.

"Old maid," mouthed Sadie. She saw the pain in Opal's eyes and wanted to apologize, but couldn't force out the words. Abruptly she turned away to stare at the vast prairie stretching on and on and on without anything else in sight.

She saw a rider to the right of the wagon, peered closer, and saw it was Riley on York's big bay. York had given Riley a change of his clothes as well as a wide-brimmed hat so that he'd look like a rancher instead of a farmer. Riley wore them with pride. Working with cattle and horses had always been his dream while he'd plowed fields for corn and wheat with Pa. Wind flapped Riley's loose shirt and the bay's long tail. Sadie waved, and Riley waved back. He was tall for sixteen and straight and tough as leather, Pa used to say.

Someone bumped against Sadie, and she glanced back to see Web and Helen still flushed from their sleep. Both had wide blue eyes, and both were whipcord thin and just as strong. She moved closer to Tanner to make room for Web and Helen. They must not see Tanner and tell York or Momma!

"Who'd you wave at, Sadie?" asked Helen.

"Yes, who?" Web leaned over the end-gate. "Oh, it's Riley!" Web's dark hair hung almost in his eyes because Momma hadn't had time to cut it and Sadie had been too angry to volunteer.

Helen's hair, almost white in its lightness, curled around her face and hung in thin braids to her shoulders. "It's Riley!" echoed Helen.

Web leaned over the end-gate and shouted, "Riley, take me with you!"

Sadie grabbed him and hauled him back inside before the wind whipped him out. "Webster! You know he can't take you. Momma said he couldn't."

"That was before." Web pulled away and scrambled over Opal's feet to reach the front of the wagon. He stood quietly, and Sadie knew he was waiting to speak. He knew he was never to interrupt adults while they were talking, no matter how excited he was. Finally he said, "Momma, can I ride with Riley? Please?"

"Let the boy ride," said York.

"You can ride," said Momma.

Sadie pressed her lips tightly together. Momma always did what York wanted. But then, that was Momma's way. She'd always done what Pa wanted to do. Momma had said many times, "The man is the head of the house, and what he says goes." If there was one egg left, Pa always got it for his breakfast. If Pa wanted to go visiting and everyone else wanted to go on a picnic, they'd go visiting. If Pa wanted to read a book, even if someone else had already started it and held it in his or her hands, Pa got to read it.

Once Sadie had asked why Pa always got his own way and Momma had said, "That's just the way it is."

Now Momma would say the same about York.

"Riley, take Web on with you," York called in his slow Texas drawl.

"Come on, Web!" Riley rode close to the wagon, making sure he didn't get tangled in Bossie's rope, and Sadie handed Web out. Riley swung him easily to the back of the saddle, and Web clung to his older brother's waist. Wind flung Web's hair back from his small face.

"Web! Riley!" Helen leaned out and waved wildly.

"Helen!" Sadie hauled her back.

"Yahoo!" shouted Web with his head back.

"Be careful, Web," Sadie called.

"He will. I'll watch out for him," Riley shouted impatiently.

"I want to ride too," said Helen with a small pout that made Sadie realize that often they babied Helen and let her have her own way.

"You can't ride," said Opal. "Momma said when you got up I was supposed to help you with your quilt block."

Helen wrinkled her nose, but she didn't argue back. Sadie knew that when she was Helen's age she wasn't allowed to wrinkle her nose over a job she didn't like. Yes, Helen was indeed spoiled.

"You're a naughty girl, Helen," Sadie said sharply.

Helen's face crumpled, but she didn't cry. In a tiny voice she said, "I'm not naughty."

"Stop it, Sadie," snapped Opal.

Sadie scowled at Opal for interfering. "She wrinkled her nose."

"Did you wrinkle your nose, Helen?" Opal asked.

Helen barely nodded.

Opal slipped her arm around Helen and kissed her pink cheek. "Don't do it again, Helen."

"I'll try not to."

Opal looked over at Sadie with a stern look. "And don't you tell her she's naughty."

Sadie lifted her round chin, and her eyes darkened. Why couldn't Opal understand that she *must* teach Helen? Pa had been strict and stern and Momma hadn't. She let the kids get by with too much, Pa had said often. "I'm only helping her to grow up to be a fine young lady, just the way Pa would want her to be."

Opal shook her finger at Sadie. "You know Momma told you to stop trying to do Pa's job for him. It's not up to you. She said York is our pa now, and he'll do it."

Sadie turned away, her sharp white teeth clamped down hard on her lower lip.

3

The Soddy

Sadie breathed a sigh of relief when York stopped the covered wagon outside his house. For almost an hour she'd guarded Tanner to keep his presence a secret. He'd not moved or made a sound.

"Here it is," said York, "our place—the Circle Y Ranch."

"We're here!" cried Helen, scrambling to the back.

Sadie peeked out and almost gasped. "It's a sod house!"

"Sod!" Opal leaped to the opening. "How can we live in a soddy?"

Sadie had been in a sod house when she'd visited the Larsens, and she'd been glad that she lived in a frame house. Grace Larsen told her about the dirt falling on her food if they didn't keep sheeting draped across the ceiling.

Helen dropped to the grass and ran to the door.

Momma said, "Oh, my. I didn't know you lived in a sod house, York."

"Didn't I mention that? Nebraska marble." York pulled off his hat and rubbed his damp hair. "When I can I'll build us a frame house."

"It's so . . . small," said Momma in a strange voice.

"Is it? I hadn't noticed."

"How will we all fit?"

"The kids could sleep in the wagon if that'd be better."

Momma patted her warm cheeks with her handkerchief. "We'll manage. Let's get the wagon unloaded."

Suddenly remembering Tanner, a muscle jumped in Sadie's cheek, and she dropped from the wagon. "Why don't you look in the house first, Momma? I can start taking out some of our things."

Momma nodded, and she walked slowly into the soddy with York, Opal, and Helen close behind her. Riley and Web leaped off the bay and ran inside after them.

Quickly Sadie uncovered Tanner, and her heart almost stopped. The pup lay barely breathing. She took out the end-gate and eased Tanner forward. Carefully she picked him up and laid him on the grass in the shade of the wagon, but he didn't move. A shadow fell across her, and she looked up to find York standing over her. The very breath in her body seemed to freeze.

"What have we here?" York hunkered down beside the dog and gently ran his hands over him. "Where'd you come from, boy?"

Sadie swallowed hard.

"You look done in, feller."

"I brought him from town!" burst out Sadie. Almost in one breath she told him about the old man and all that had happened. "And I want to doctor Tanner back to health."

York studied her a long time and finally he winked. "I reckon you should get some water down him first, and then food if he'll take it."

Sadie looked around, saw the covered well, and ran to draw a bucket of water. Tanner swallowed a little before his head flopped down. She stayed beside him a few more minutes, then walked back to unload the wagon.

Whistling, Riley led the team to the sod barn, with Web, also whistling, trailing along with Bossie. The sun was low, and Bossie mooed to remind them that it was past milking time.

Wind blowing her dress around her slender body, Opal carried water to the house to help Momma scrub the dishes and the cooking pots.

York unlatched the water barrel and stood it beside the well. His knife handle stuck out of the leather sheath on his hip. It was as much a part of him as his hat and the pistol on his other hip. He helped Sadie lift out the supplies. "Leave the clothes in the wagon until I put up shelves and pegs."

Sadie nodded and pushed the wooden boxes against the pile of quilts that they were leaving in until they could decide the sleeping arrangements for the night.

Her sunbonnet flopping on her back and her cheeks pink, Helen ran to Sadie. She spotted Tanner, bent to pet him and ask about him, then said before Sadie could answer, "Momma says to help me get fuel."

Sadie looked around, but couldn't see the usual stack of wood that they'd always had beside their house in Douglas County. The wagon, the barn with a barbed-wire corral on one side of it, a small outhouse, and the sod house stood all alone in the middle of a vast wilderness of waving grasses, dotted with small spring flowers. Finally she turned to York. "Where's the wood?"

"To burn? There ain't one stick to be had. But I have plenty of Nebraska coal." His blue eyes twinkled as he motioned toward the prairie.

"Come on, Helen. He means buffalo chips and cow chips." Sadie lifted two buckets off the side of the wagon and handed one to Helen.

"I'm going to get us some rabbits or prairie chickens for supper," said York, mounting the bay.

Sadie nodded and walked away with Helen.

"Make sure I don't get one that's not dry," said Helen, half-carrying, half-dragging her bucket.

"Just remember to pick them up by the edge and if you see the middle is still wet, drop them back for us to get when they are dry." Sadie couldn't remember a time when she hadn't helped pick up dried manure for fuel. She knew Helen had started helping when she was two years old.

A snake slithered across in front of Helen. She stopped until it was out of her way and then continued, all the time chattering about the dog.

Sadie answered her questions, and had to tell the story twice about Ty Bailer as they searched in the grass for chips. "I think York will let me keep Tanner." He hadn't said so, but he hadn't said she couldn't either.

"Will you let me pet him?"

"Yes."

"Thanks." Helen smiled at Sadie, then bent to pick up another cow chip. She dropped it, turned her face away, and rubbed her fingers on her apron. "It wasn't dry."

A distant shot rang out, then two more and Sadie knew York had shot supper for them.

"My bucket's full." Sadie stood with her face to the wind to dry her perspiration. "Can you fit more in yours, Helen?"

"A little." Helen ran here and there, picking up the flat, dry chips. When her bucket was full, she gripped the handle and waited for Sadie.

With her left hand Sadie helped carry Helen's bucket and with her right carried her own. Wind flapped her dress around her thin legs and pushed her bonnet between her sharp shoulder blades. Sometimes she felt like the wind would pick her up and carry her off, just like it did the tumbleweeds in the fall.

"Could I feed Tanner once in a while, Sadie?"

"Yes."

"And water him?"

"Yes."

"I could teach him tricks."

"I'll let you."

Helen smiled a pleased little smile, and Sadie felt good all over.

"Let's pick a bouquet of flowers for Momma for the table," said Sadie.

They set the buckets down and quickly picked the small purple and white and blue flowers, sniffing the beautiful aroma that for a moment was stronger than the soil and the still-wet cow chips. Birds flew around them happily. When a coyote yapped in the distance, Helen proudly carried the bouquet in her free hand as they walked as fast as they could back to the house.

Just as they reached the yard Sadie saw York ride in with three rabbits dangling from the side of the saddle. They looked soft and sweet, and for a minute she hated the thought of eating them.

Riley ran from the house with Web at his heels. "I'll skin them, York," Riley said, reaching for the rabbits.

"Me too," said Web.

"We'll do it together," said York. He swung his leg over the saddle and dropped to the ground in one easy motion. "Web, water Bay and take her to the corral."

Web took the reins and walked away. One step and the big bay could've flattened him like a pancake, but Sadie knew York had trained her well.

Momma stood in the doorway of the house and called, "Girls, bring in the fuel. The fire's low."

Sadie and Helen walked as fast as they could to the house with the buckets. Heat struck Sadie, and she wanted to go back out into the cool wind. She blinked to accustom her eyes to the darkness and saw Opal at the window, looking out.

The smell of cornbread made Sadie hungry. They set the buckets beside the black cast-iron stove that stood out from the sod wall. A piece of once white sheeting hung on the ceiling over the stove to keep dirt and bugs from falling into the food being cooked. A lamp burned on the shelf beside the stove, casting enough light to cook by. Light from the window and door was quickly swallowed by the dark room. Momma opened the stove and dropped in two chips. Flames leaped high, and she quickly dropped the lid in place.

Helen hurried to the door, saying over her thin shoulder, "I'm going to watch York and Riley skin the rabbits."

"Don't get blood on your clothes," warned Momma.

"I won't." The words floated back into the house, but were swallowed up by the thick walls.

Opal walked to the door. "Call me when you need me, Momma."

"I will."

Sadie slowly turned and looked around the room. It would be impossible for seven people to sleep without taking up all the walk space. There was no bed, and the table was made of sod. It was covered with Momma's embroidered tablecloth. Two wooden chairs stood beside the table, and Sadie knew she and the other children would kneel on the floor to eat— unless they ate outdoors on the ground. A bucket of water with a dipper in it and a washbasin stood on a sod stand. One of Momma's towels lay behind the basin. A guitar hung by a wide leather strap on a peg next to the window, with a pair of pants and a shirt on another peg.

York's home.

And now theirs.

"We'll make it do, Sadie," said Momma softly.

Sadie nodded. They always did. "I'll be outside if you need me, Momma."

"I gave your dog another drink while you were gone."

"Thank you." Sadie smiled, and Momma nodded before she turned back to her work.

Outdoors Sadie sat beside Tanner while the others watched York stretch the rabbit hides over slabs of wood, the soft fur inside and the greasy skin out. He stood them up on a shelf outside the sod barn to dry.

Sadie gave Tanner another swallow of water. "I'll bring you something to eat after supper, Tanner." She was sure she saw a tiny flicker of his tail. "Good boy, Tanner."

A few minutes later Sadie rolled the rabbit in flour and fried it crisp in lard while Momma made good thick gravy.

Opal and Helen set the table with Momma's dishes and filled the glasses with milk that Web had taken from Bossie. When the food was on, Momma sent Helen to call York and the boys.

"And tell Web to wash his hands clean," Sadie called after Helen.

When York walked in, Momma looked at him as if she hadn't seen him in days. He hugged her and even kissed her cheek right in front of everyone. Sadie looked quickly away.

"York, you and I will sit here," said Momma, touching the chairs that sat side by side. "Riley, Web, Opal, Helen, and Sadie there." Momma pointed to each place and Riley, Opal and Sadie knelt at the table, but Web and Helen were short enough to stand.

"I see I'll have to make us some benches," said York.

"I'll help you," said Riley.

Sadie knew that Riley would walk barefoot on cactus to help York since he'd given him the rancher clothes and the wide-brimmed hat.

"We'll do it, Riley." York's even white teeth flashed in his sun-darkened face as he smiled. He looked around the table. "This is a happy day for me. Let's pray."

Sadie bowed her head, and once again she was

forced to listen to another man besides Pa pray over the food.

"Our Father God, thank You for bringin' us safe to our home. Thank You for this fine family, for my dear wife, and thank You for this good-smellin' food set before us. It's blessed in Jesus' name. Amen."

Sadie liked the prayer, but liking it made her feel guilty and she determined that she would eat just enough to keep Momma from asking her what was wrong.

Momma handed York the plate of steaming hot rabbit. He took it and held it toward her. She looked at him questioningly and he said, "You take what you want, Bess."

Momma hesitated and finally took one small piece. York forked another one beside that, then held the plate out to Opal, then Sadie, Helen and the boys.

Sadie knew her eyes were wide with surprise, but she didn't say anything and neither did the others. They all knew that children at the table were to be seen and not heard. None of them could speak unless they were asked a question.

York passed around the gravy and the cornbread before he helped himself. Finally he sat back and looked at the children. Sadie wanted to slip out of sight, but she managed to return his look. "Why are you kids suddenly so quiet?"

Momma's eyebrows raised up almost to her dark hair. "York, didn't you know that children shouldn't talk at the table?"

"No, I didn't know that. I guess bein' an orphan kept me from learnin' such rules." He laughed. "If you don't mind, I'd like to have us talk at the table."

Sadie couldn't bring herself to, and neither did the others unless York or Momma spoke to them.

In the silence Sadie heard a noise behind her.
York leaped to his feet, his hand over the knife that he
always carried at his side. "Don't move."

Sadie wanted to ask what was wrong, but she
knew that they shouldn't say or do anything to dis-
tract York. She watched as he suddenly struck out
with his knife. She looked down to see the blade stick-
ing through a writhing rattlesnake and into the dirt
floor. Sadie shuddered.

"So much for that," said York. He cut off the
rattles, stuck his knife back in its sheath, and flung the
snake out the door. "We'll skin it later, boys." He
looked at the piece in his hand. "Four rattles. Only a
small one." He dropped the rattles inside his guitar,
shook it, and said, "That's five now."

Sadie stared at York for a long time, just as the
others were doing.

"Oh my," said Momma.

Later Sadie carried a piece of cornbread soaked
in gravy to Tanner. Weakly he ate it, drummed his tail
twice, and lay still.

"You keep doctorin' him and he'll make it, Sadie
Rose."

Sadie glanced up as York squatted down beside
her. He always called her Sadie Rose, even though she
kept telling him she was called only Sadie. He said
that's how it was done in Texas. He said girls always
went by two names. She'd told him that wasn't the
way it was in Nebraska, but he said, "You can take a
man out of Texas, but you can't take Texas out of a
man."

"But you're a Nebraska man now."

"I got a heart big enough to hold Texas and
Nebraska both, Sadie Rose. And there's room for you
too."

She pushed the thoughts away as she watched York study Tanner.

"He looks better already, Sadie Rose."

Tanner lifted his head, and she laid it in her lap and stroked his matted hair. "You look better already, Tanner," she said, gently echoing York's words.

4

The Garden

Sadie opened her eyes and listened. What had wakened her? Warm and snug under a feather tick and two quilts, Opal and Helen slept beside her at the front of the covered wagon, while Riley and Web slept at the back with another feather tick and quilts. Riley snored, and Sadie wondered if that's what she'd heard.

She peeked over the wagon seat and saw the pink shades of dawn. Birds twittered their usual waking sounds. A horse nickered.

Slowly, carefully Sadie pulled off her nightcap and eased off her nightdress, then slipped on her clothes. Silently she climbed over the seat and dropped to the dewy grass. It was cold and wet against her bare feet.

Shivering from the morning chill, she ran first to the one-hole outhouse and then to the barn where she'd put Tanner for the night. The hard-packed floor of the barn felt warm. She liked the pleasant odor of sod and animals. She lit the lantern that York kept on a peg beside the door, careful to use only one match. She turned the wick low to conserve coal oil and to keep the glass from turning black with soot.

Shadows flickered as she walked to the dark corner where she'd laid Tanner last night, set the lantern on the floor, and knelt beside the dog. "How are you this morning?"

He whined and moved his tail slightly. She stroked him and talked softly to him about how he was going to get well and run after rabbits and play with her.

Bossie bawled in the corral. The horses nickered. Momma's voice barely reached her as she called for everyone to get up and around. As if it were yesterday she could hear Pa shouting, "The sun's up, you kids. How come you're still in bed?"

"Oh, Pa," she whispered with a break in her voice.

She blew out the lantern, hung it back in place, and ran to the house.

Later she coaxed Tanner to eat the breakfast cornbread she'd baked, covered with grease from the salt pork Opal had fried. Tanner sniffed and finally swallowed a few bites.

Outdoors the sun was barely peeking over the top of the eastern prairie. Already Sadie had helped Helen fold the quilts they'd used in the wagon, had eaten breakfast, and had strained the milk that Web brought in from Bossie. Opal had mixed up bread and set it to rise, while Momma talked to York about the garden they were to plant before sunset. With all of them helping, she'd said they should get done.

Webster ran into the barn and stopped beside Sadie. "He's my dog too, Sadie. Momma said so. She told York if you get to keep the dog, then it should be for all of us, not just you."

Sadie caught Web by the front of his worn shirt. "Don't you dare tell me he's your dog too!"

Web's mouth dropped open, and he stared at Sadie as if she was a stranger. "But . . . but York said . . ."

"I don't care what York said! Tanner is *my* dog!"

Anger flared in Web's blue eyes, and he kicked Sadie in the shin.

She yelped and hopped around on one leg. "Ouch! You bad boy! That hurt! I'm gonna get you for that!"

Now he grabbed her braid and yanked hard.

Tears burned her eyes as she rubbed her head.

"I'm almost as big as you, Sadie, so don't you try anything with me!"

She glared at him and finally turned away. He was strong, and he wouldn't let her hurt him without hurting her back. "I'm takin' Tanner outdoors for fresh air, and you better stay out of my way, Webster!"

"Let me help, Sadie."

"Get away from my dog!"

"He's my dog too. York and Momma said so!"

Sadie eased Tanner up and tried to get him to walk, but he was too weak. She picked him up and carried him out to a nest of grass where he'd slept before. The sun felt warm after being inside the cool sod barn.

"Here's the water." Web splashed some on his pant leg as he set the bucket beside his sister.

The anger oozed out of Sadie, and she stepped away from Tanner. "You can water him if you want to, Web."

Web poured water in a dish and held it close to Tanner's nose. Finally he lapped the water. "You're a good dog, Tanner." Web leaned down and kissed Tanner's face. "Sadie, I'll ask York if he has a brush we can use on him. He'd feel better with his coat smooth." Web jerked his head to toss his hair out of his eyes, and a pang of guilt stabbed Sadie.

"Web, if we have time today I'll cut your hair."

He looked at her for a long time. "I guess I'll let you." Web pushed back his hair with both hands, but it flopped back down. "Opal said she'd braid it if I didn't do something with it."

"You might look cute with braids."

Web scowled. "I'll never let Opal cut my hair again."

Sadie laughed and felt all her anger toward Web fade away. She knew he wasn't mad at her any longer, and she was glad. She glanced across the yard and saw Momma motion to them to come. "Momma's ready to plant the garden. Let's go." Sadie patted Tanner one last time and ran to Momma as she walked across the yard with York.

Momma was saying, "It will work, York. I know it's a little late for peas and potatoes, but we'll plant them anyway."

"I never put in a garden before, Bess, but your word's good enough for me. I'll leave Riley to plow, but when he's done I'll need his help. I told him I'd ride Bay and he could use Dick and Jane."

Sadie looked across the yard where Riley already had York's horses hooked to the plow. Knowing York had given them names made her feel warm and soft inside.

"Fresh vegetables will taste good, Bess. You're a wonder," said York.

Sadie knew Momma could raise anything. She said she'd learned it when she was a little girl in Michigan. Then, when they'd moved to Nebraska they'd learned the new growing season, and she'd raised the best garden around. When she married Pa, he always bragged on her garden. Anytime someone visited Momma she always showed off her garden, exclaiming over every plant as if there weren't any like it in all the world. And when Momma visited her friends they always did the same. Momma had always been quick to say their gardens were beautiful and well-tended.

York called to Web, and when Web reached his side York said, "You take your momma's cow out in the grass over there and stake her out on the picket line." While they were still in Douglas County Sadie had heard Momma tell York that she couldn't do without the cow, without milk and cream, cheese and butter. No, she couldn't do without her milk cow. And York had said that even if it was hard, they'd tie Bossie to the back of the wagon and take her west with them. He hadn't complained once, and Momma had been pleased to have her own way.

York ruffled Web's hair. "Be sure Bossie gets watered enough. And when she eats all the grass off, you move her."

Web nodded and smiled, but he didn't ask why she couldn't stay in the corral. He knew as well as Sadie did that he was never to question what an adult said. He ran to get the stake and picket line.

Sadie knew Bossie was to have a calf any day now, and she knew Momma was hoping for a heifer calf. Momma said if they had two cows to milk, they could sell the extra butter and have cash money. Cash money was hard to come by.

Once Sadie had had five pennies of her very own, but that was the most she'd ever had. Riley had earned one whole dollar when he'd worked for a farmer during wheat harvest. Riley had held on to the dollar to save it for a special thing, but then he had to give it to Momma to help with Pa's funeral.

Sadie jumped at the sound of her name and forced the knot out of her stomach. Someday she'd pay back that dollar to Riley, and then he could save it for something special.

"Sadie, stop wool gathering," said Momma with a frown. "I have spoken to you twice."

"Sorry, Momma."

York turned to Sadie. "Saddle Bay for me, Sadie Rose. Give him a long drink of water before you bring him to me."

Sadie nodded and ran to get the big bay from the corral. She crawled through the fence and called to Bay, and he trotted to her and stood still while she slipped on the bridle. She led him out of the corral to the barn door, flung the saddle blanket across Bay's back, and then swung the saddle in place. She tightened the cinch strap and led Bay to the well, where Helen had water waiting.

York thanked Sadie, kissed Momma good-bye, and rode away, tall in the saddle. As Sadie watched him, he grew smaller and smaller until the prairie swallowed him up. A loneliness rose up inside her that she couldn't understand. Slowly she turned to follow Momma to where Opal stood with the potatoes.

Across the yard Riley walked behind the horses with the plow. But he was plowing *inside* the corral.

Sadie ran forward yelling, "Riley, get out of the corral with that plow!"

Riley turned his head, turned back, and kept going.

"Sadie!" shouted Momma.

At the sharp sound of Momma's call Sadie turned and walked back. Why did Momma look so upset?

"Sadie, you stop that! I told Riley to plow the corral for the garden. That ground is already free of grassy roots and will make a better garden than the prairie."

Sadie hung her head. How she hated to be scolded! "I'm sorry, Momma."

"As well you should be." Momma turned away. "Now let's get the potatoes cut."

Sadie rubbed her hands across her apron and followed Momma.

Before it was time to make dinner, Riley had the spot plowed for the garden. While Opal and Helen chattered to Momma and Web watered Bossie, Sadie sat back and looked at the piles of potato eyes that they had cut. Each potato had to be cut into pieces so that each piece had at least three eyes. The eyes grew into new potato plants that would grow under the ground and become big potatoes that they'd dig up in the fall. They'd store the potatoes in a cool place under the ground and eat them all winter, saving enough to plant the next spring. Each year as long as Sadie could remember it was the same. She knew that each year as long as Momma could remember it had been the same too.

After dinner Sadie stopped to water and feed Tanner and move him to the shade of the house, while Riley took the plow to the ground outside the corral that Momma had marked off for sod corn and more potatoes. Momma had said sod corn and potatoes could push through the thick grass and still produce. By next year the ground would be easier to plow, and with another year the ground would be a field and not open pastureland. After that they'd have to leave it alone so the loose soil wouldn't blow away. Another spot would have to be used for planting.

Web jabbed Sadie's arm. "Momma's calling you."

"Oh." Sadie patted Tanner one last time and ran to the garden with Web close on her heels. The ground felt soft and warm to her bare feet. Birds flew around the barn. Meadowlarks sat on the prairie grasses and sang a melody so beautiful that it caught at Sadie's throat and she wanted to stop just to listen to them.

"Take the rake, Sadie," Momma said, holding it out to her. Wind blew Momma's dress against her sturdy body. She wore her old pair of shoes that once had been her good shoes. Her good shoes were in the covered wagon, wrapped carefully to protect them until York built a shelf in the house where Momma could put them. Her hands were dirty, and a smudge of dirt covered part of her left cheek. "You start on that side, and Opal will start there. I'll use the hoe to mark off the rows."

Web and Helen picked up any clumps that were there, shook them hard enough to knock out topsoil, then carried the clumps to the fence and tossed them over.

Sadie held the rake and for a minute watched Riley lean into the plow as he walked behind Dick and

Jane as they pulled the plow forward over ground that had never seen a plow before. Birds flew down and grabbed up the worms that were suddenly uncovered.

Sadie knew that Riley longed to be with York, tending the cattle and horses, but he'd known he couldn't when Momma needed him to plow.

Opal raked and talked about the new style of dresses she'd seen in the Montgomery Ward catalogue. Momma let her chatter as long as she kept working. Sadie knew Opal wouldn't get to order a dress, but she could find one she liked and sew it herself just as soon as they had cash money to spend on goods.

Sadie raked the clods into smooth soil as the hot sun burned through her sunbonnet and her dress. Wind dried the perspiration on her face and body before it soaked through her clothes.

Momma carefully dropped seeds in the rows she'd made with the hoe and gently covered them over. She marked the row with the special stakes she'd made years ago. Each wooden stake was about eight inches tall, two inches wide at the top, and whittled down to a point. The picture of a vegetable was painted on each stake at the widest part. The other end was the point, and it was to be stuck in the ground. Momma couldn't use some of them because she didn't have seed or because some had to be started in the house and then the tiny plant set out in the garden. There had been no time to plant the seeds to make tiny plants.

Sadie watched the pleased look on Momma's face as she pushed in the stake with the carrot painted on it. When it was time to weed, they'd all know what was weed and what was vegetable. Sadie couldn't remember when she didn't know the shapes of the vegetable leaves that Momma planted year after year. And she couldn't remember a time that she didn't help pull weeds and pick potato bugs and harvest the crops. During summer and fall her fingers were always stained from one kind of food or another.

For a moment she leaned on the rake to give her back and arms a rest. Momma never seemed to get tired. She worked hard, with her sunbonnet blocking her face and her solid body leaning over the row. Love welled up inside Sadie, and a lump filled her throat.

How could she survive without Momma?

Sadie turned abruptly away and raked furiously. It was her own fault that she had to leave Momma and the others. Somehow they'd survive.

"Somebody's coming, Momma," said Opal in a breathless voice.

Sadie turned to see a lone rider. She narrowed her eyes and finally recognized Levi Cass on a black mare. She smiled.

Opal's face blanched, and she gripped the rake tighter. "It's a young man, Momma! I can't let a fine young man see me with bare feet and in such a mess."

"You're a hard-working girl, Opal. You have nothing to be ashamed of," said Momma in a firm voice.

"Oh!" Opal looked wildly around, then finally tugged at her dress and retied the strings of her sunbonnet. There was nothing she could do about her dirty hands.

"It's Levi Cass, Opal. And he's coming to see me," Sadie announced.

"You?"

"You, Sadie?" echoed Momma.

Sadie nodded and with a smile stepped forward to greet her friend.

5
Levi Cass

The warm wind blew sand against Sadie as she stood at the side of the corral and watched Levi. She caught sight of the polished butt of a Winchester in the boot of the saddle before Levi swung easily out and landed on the ground with a gentle thud. The creak of the leather and the stamp of the black mare's hoof seemed loud in the sudden silence behind her in the garden. She knew Web and Helen were standing beside Momma just waiting to get permission to run to greet Levi. Opal was probably trying to rub the dirt off her hands, while she wished she could sneak to the covered wagon for her shoes.

"Hi, Levi," said Sadie with a shy smile. She liked his baggy blue shirt and the red-print bandanna tied loosely around her neck.

"Howdy, Sadie." Levi pulled off his hat, and his

brown eyes sparkled with excitement. A rim of his dark hair where his hatband had been was pressed tightly to his head. "How's Tanner?"

She had to look up some to meet his eyes. "Doin' good. Hasn't got up yet, but he wags his tail."

"Good." Levi looked over Sadie's shoulder, and she knew the exact moment he spotted Opal.

Sadie locked her hands tightly together over her dirty apron. Jealousy shot through her like she'd never felt before.

He smiled and took a step as if to go around her. "I never met your family, Sadie."

She wanted to refuse to introduce him, but she knew she couldn't. "Come on and meet them."

Levi smiled at her, then turned his look back to Opal.

Sadie wanted to throw a clod of dirt at him. But she knew she had to mind her manners, so she walked with him across the garden. "Watch so you don't step on the rows."

He skip-jumped over one and said, "Sorry. I didn't see 'em."

She stopped before Momma with Web and Helen close at her side and Opal a foot away. Helen buried her face against Momma and finally peeked out. Web studied Levi as if he wanted to memorize him. Sadie didn't dare look at Opal. "Momma, this is Levi Cass. He's the boy who helped me with Tanner, him and his pa."

"Hello, Levi. Thank you for helping Sadie." Momma smiled her slow, sweet smile. "Could I get you a drink of water or maybe something to eat?"

"Thanks, Mrs. York, not right now. It's a pleasure to meet you. We—me and Paw—have been good friends with York the two years he's had this place, and we were pleased to hear he got himself a family."

When he stopped talking Sadie said, "And this is Opal."

Levi grinned enough to split his face. "Howdy, Opal."

"It's a pleasure to meet you, Levi. I'm sorry that I'm such a mess."

Sadie doubled her fists, and before Levi could say anything more to Opal she said, "And this is Web and Helen. They been helpin' me with Tanner."

He smiled his friendly smile at them and answered their greeting, but all the time his eyes strayed to Opal. "York around?" he finally asked.

"Out checking fences and the livestock," said Momma, telling Levi the directions that York had told her. Sadie knew Momma wanted to get back to her planting, but she never let on with the polite way she spoke to Levi and the easy way she stood.

"Paw sent me here to help York today." Levi worried the brim of his hat that he held in his big suntanned hands. "York sold us a mare in December, and I'm working it off since we had no ready cash to pay him."

"I'm sure he appreciates your help," said Opal.

Sadie bit her lip, and shot a look at Opal that she ignored.

Levi smiled again at Opal. "I best be gettin' out to him before much more of the day is gone."

"It was nice to meet you, Levi," said Momma.

"My pleasure, Mrs. York." Levi turned to Opal. "A real pleasure, Opal."

"I hope you come when you can visit with us longer," said Opal. Sadie knew the "us" meant "me."

"I'll do that." Levi clamped his hat on his head and turned away, then turned back and grinned at

Sadie. "I reckon I can spare a minute to check on Tanner, if it's all right with you."

Sadie turned to Momma. "Can I show Levi the dog, Momma? I'll be real quick."

Momma nodded. "And give Levi and his horse a drink."

"I will."

"Appreciate it," said Levi with one last smile at Opal.

With Levi beside her, Sadie walked away from the garden, away from Opal's glow of beauty, and toward the welcome shade of the barn. She didn't speak until they reached Tanner. "He ate this morning, Levi. And he drank more than yesterday. He still can't stand up alone."

Levi knelt beside Tanner and gently ran his hands over him, just like York had done. "No broken bones. But he's been treated real bad for a long time. It's a wonder he don't snap at us for touchin' him."

"I think he knows we're helpin' him." Sadie stroked Tanner's head. "His eyes are clearer, so I think he's in less pain than he was." Her face hardened. "That mean Ty Bailer!"

"He's a mean one, all right. You're brave for standin' up to him the way you did."

His words pleased her and almost took away the ache that he'd caused by his attention to Opal. "I just didn't want Tanner to die." Her voice cracked on the last word. She was quiet a long time. "My pa died."

"I wondered."

"Froze in a blizzard."

"That's too bad."

She nodded. Levi would probably hate her as much as she hated herself if he knew she'd caused Pa's death. "It's been real hard without Pa."

"Now you have York. He's a good man."

Sadie nodded.

"He's teachin' me about horses, and one of these days I'm goin' to be as good as he is on one." Levi sat back on the high heels of his boots, and his face flushed with excitement. "York can rope a steer at a full gallop. He can cut better than anybody I ever saw."

"Cut?"

"You know. Cut the steer out of a herd that he's after."

"Oh." They'd never owned more than Bossie, her calf, and a steer for beef.

"That York can stay on a buckin' horse until it's worn right out and knows who's boss. I reckon he's the best cowpoke in all of Nebraska."

Sadie moved restlessly. She'd heard enough about York. "Momma needs my help, Levi. I think I'd better get back to work. Will you come again soon?"

"Tomorrow, if it's all right with Paw."

She walked him to the well and watched as he pulled up water for his horse and filled a dipper for himself. At a sound behind her Sadie turned to find Riley standing there covered with dirt from head to toe. His eyelashes were gray with dust.

Levi turned, then held the dipper of cold water out to Riley. He took it and drank deeply.

"Riley, this is Levi Cass." The smell of Riley's sweat stung Sadie's nose. "He came to help York."

"Hi." Riley shook hands with Levi.

"I noticed you plowin'." Levi pushed his hat back. "I never did have to plow."

Sadie saw a muscle jump in Riley's jaw. She knew how badly he wanted to be away from the plow and out helping York.

"It's hard work."

"I can see that. It was nice meetin' you, Riley."
Levi fairly leaped into the saddle, waved to Opal, and
said, "See you tomorrow, Sadie."

"Yes." She watched him ride away in a cloud of
dust.

"Never learned to plow," muttered Riley. He
slapped dust off his sleeves and shirtfront, and Sadie
sneezed. "Wish I could say the same. If Momma
didn't need my help, I'd be out with York right now
and he'd have no use for Levi's help."

"Levi traded help for a horse."

"I still wish I was out with York." Riley drank
another dipper of water, hung it in place, and strode
away.

Sadie sighed and finally walked back to take up
her rake.

"I'd like boots like Levi's," said Web, watching
the speck on the prairie that was Levi.

"Me too," said Helen.

"He's handsome," said Opal.

"He's not old enough to get married," snapped
Sadie.

"I only said he was handsome."

"But you're already tryin' your name out with
his. Opal Cass. Mrs. Levi Cass."

"I am not!"

"I bet you are!"

"Girls," said Momma in her warning voice, and
Sadie knew she had to watch her tone and not be
rude.

"I'm sorry, Sadie," said Opal, her cheeks flushed
and her eyes flashing.

Sadie bit her tongue and leaned low over her

rake, raking so hard the wind carried her dust away in little dust devils.

"Tell her you're sorry, Sadie," said Momma.

Sadie's jaw tightened, but finally she said in a low, tight voice, "I'm sorry, Opal."

Tears smarted her eyes as she raked faster. Now's when she should ask Momma to let her go back to Douglas County, she thought, now when it would be easy for Momma to say yes.

Momma picked up a stone about the size of her thumbnail and held it in the palm of her callused hand. "You children should see the rocks in Michigan."

Sadie knew that meant it was time for a break, and she leaned against the rake and watched Momma's face. She always got that special look when she talked about her childhood in Michigan, and Sadie knew her mother missed the trees and the cool summer nights and her lake just down a hill from her house that she fished and swam in during the summers and ice-skated on during the winters.

"What were the rocks like, Momma?" asked Helen, peering at the stone in Momma's hand.

Momma leaned down and kissed Helen's cheek. "When I was your age I had a wooden boat that I pulled to the garden."

"A boat, Momma?" asked Opal as if she couldn't believe she'd heard right.

Momma pushed back her sunbonnet and nodded. "It was made of wood and had wide wooden runners and was called a stoneboat."

"What did you do with it?" asked Web.

"I loaded it with stones and pulled it from the garden to dump the stones on the stone pile. If I got it too full, my brother George would help me pull it."

Sadie looked at the stone in Momma's hand. "It would take a long time to make a whole pile, Momma."

She laughed, and her cheeks turned pink and her dark eyes sparkled. Sadie loved to hear her laugh. "In Papa's garden the stones were big. I picked up stones that I could barely lift onto the stoneboat."

Opal frowned slightly. "Momma?"

"It's the truth, Opal." Momma measured with her hands, hands that had moved stones and planted gardens and tended babies. "Some of the stones were this big. And some of them in the field were so big Papa had to plow around them because he couldn't move them even with help from the team."

Sadie tried to picture stones that big, but try as she might she couldn't do it. The biggest one she'd ever seen was the size of a walnut.

"How did the stones get there?" asked Helen as she stroked the rock in her hand.

Momma shook her head. "Papa asked the same thing, and so did I. They were just there and no matter how many I picked up, more came."

Web looked around at the sandy garden. "We don't have stones like that in ours."

"No, not in Nebraska," said Momma. She smiled at each of them and motioned toward the well. "Let's go for a nice cold drink of water and sit in the shade a while." Momma laid her hoe down and walked carefully over her rows, with Helen and Web on either side of her.

Sadie dropped her rake, the tines down, and ran after them.

"Sadie. Wait."

She turned to wait for Opal.

"Is Levi coming tomorrow?" whispered Opal.

The rosy feeling of sharing some of Momma's past filled Sadie, and she nodded without the sharp pang of jealousy shooting through her.

"Good." Opal played with her bonnet strings. "I like him."

"Me too."

"I think he likes me."

"He likes me too."

Opal gasped. "You're too young to have a young man court you."

Sadie's eyes widened. "Court me? No young man is gonna court me ever!"

"Here's water, girls," called Momma.

Sadie dashed across the yard, her heels flying and her skirts flapping around her bony legs.

6

The Tree

"I brought you something, Bess." York stood just inside the door of the soddy and smiled at Momma, cooking mush on the stove.

Sadie watched York, then Momma, then bent over the soft biscuit dough she was patting out to cut into nice, round biscuits with the tin cup Momma always used. First she'd dip the rim of the tin cup in flour, and then she'd set it in a spot on the dough so as not to waste any, and then press until the cup cut through the dough. She'd lift the biscuit off the table and set it on the baking pan tight against a corner, so that each biscuit would be pushed against the other. When they rose from the heat of the oven, they'd puff up and up until they were tall, soft, delicious biscuits to eat with gravy or butter and jam.

"What do you have for me, York?"

"Come and see."

Sadie heard the happiness in Momma's voice, and she struggled against the ache inside. At that moment, she couldn't remember hearing any happiness in Momma's voice when she had talked to Pa. Did she love York more than she had Pa?

York pulled Momma to him, kissed her, and took her outdoors, but not before Sadie saw the flush of pleasure on her face. Sadie couldn't remember, in the years Momma and Pa had been married, seeing Pa kiss her. Momma had said that Pa didn't believe in showing affection in front of others. York wasn't that way. When he felt like kissing Momma, he'd do it, even if the little ones were watching.

Sadie walked to the wide window and peeked out.

"I wonder what he has for her," said Opal.

"I know what it is," said Web.

"You do not!" Sadie turned on Web and scowled. "How can you know?"

"I helped him get it this morning."

"So did I," said Helen, though she really hadn't. When she'd come in the house from the wagon with a runny nose, Momma had put her to bed on the straw tick that she and York shared. Momma didn't want to take any chances on her getting sick again the way she was a few months ago.

"What is it?" asked Opal.

Web puffed up his thin chest with pride. "I ain't tellin'."

"You can't say 'ain't' and you know it," snapped Sadie.

"York does," said Web. "Ain't. Ain't. Ain't!" With each word he stepped closer to Sadie, until he almost yelled the last word in her face.

She grabbed for him, but he was quicker and jumped out of her reach, almost falling into the biscuits. Sadie let him go, wiped her hands on her apron, and said, "I'm goin' out to look."

"Oh no, you're not!" cried Opal. "This is a romantic time for them, and you are goin' to leave them alone!"

Sadie scowled even harder now. The heat pressed against her, stifling her. The smell of mush drifted out to cover the smell of the biscuit dough. She pushed the pan of biscuits into the oven, added one cow chip, and slid the stove lid back in place.

Web stood at the door with his hands in front of his bib overalls. "York said I could take you all out after he showed Momma. He showed her, so you can all come."

"Me too," said Helen. She scrambled off the tick, her cheeks flushed and her hair frizzy without Momma's hand to braid it.

Sadie hung back as the girls ran after Web. Finally she couldn't stand it. She ran after them and stopped on the south side of the house. A tall tree stood several feet from the house—the only tree on the whole homestead, maybe in the whole county. Sadie saw a pleased, proud look on York's face.

Momma stood beside the tree, her cheek against the bark and her hand caressing the lowest branch. The trunk was no bigger around than her wrist. Its tiny leaves, higher than her head, waved in the breeze.

"Isn't it a beautiful tree, children? It's an oak just like the one that stood in my yard when I was a youngster in Michigan."

Sadie thought of the many stories Momma had told about the land in Michigan. She'd said that as far as the eye could see there were trees. Trees of all kinds. Trees so big around, three men couldn't reach around them. Sadie had tried to imagine what it would be like to see trees everywhere, but try as hard as she could, she couldn't imagine it. When she closed her eyes she saw grasses waving in the wind or corn-fields or wheat fields, and a blue sky bigger than all of the fields, but she couldn't see more than one or two trees in any one place. The one time she'd seen the Missouri River she'd seen a long row of trees that followed it along, but no trees spread out over the land. If she hadn't known that Momma never lied, she'd have thought Momma was lying about all those trees.

Momma had said that Christmas trees grew ev-erywhere, and her papa would take them all into the forest to choose a tree. She'd said there were hun-dreds to choose from, and the needles were long and soft and didn't prick your hand when you decorated them the way the scraggly cedar trees did that they'd used for Nebraska Christmas trees.

For the first time Sadie thought about Christmas, and she wondered where they'd find even a cedar tree for this Christmas. Maybe York could find a cedar since he could find an oak.

"We'll have to water the tree every morning and every night," said Momma, still stroking the trunk.

"I'll water it," said Web.

"Me too," said Helen. She touched a tiny leaf in awe.

"Birds will build nests in it," said Momma.

"Someday this tree will shade the yard, and we'll put a bench under it to sit and rest on," said York. "We'll buy lumber and build us a two-story frame house with lots of room. And we'll plant more trees—

just like this one. We'll have so many tress that you won't be able to see the pasture."

Momma walked to York and slipped her arms around him and kissed him right on the mouth.

Sadie looked quickly away. Momma had never, ever done that to Pa in front of anyone. She heard Opal sigh, and she glanced at her and frowned. Opal thought Momma and York were very "romantic."

Just then Riley ran up, red and panting. "York, Dick and Jane got spooked by a rabbit and ran before I could hook up the plow. I tried to catch 'em, but couldn't."

"Don't let it worry you none, pard. They're a skittish pair, but they'll come to me once they've had their run." York clamped a hand on Riley's shoulder. "Dick and Jane like their time of play." York touched Momma's cheek. "Keep breakfast warm for me." He ran across the yard where his big bay stood and leaped into the saddle without touching a boot to the stirrup.

Riley sighed and shook his head. "I tried to catch them, Momma."

"I know you did, son." Momma squeezed Riley's hand, and he flushed with pleasure.

"I'll plow for you, Riley," said Sadie.

He looked at her and shook his head. "Wait'll you have a little growth on you, and then maybe you can."

Sadie sighed. "Momma, will I ever grow big?"

"Your Grandma Keller didn't reach five feet, so you might stay just the little mite you are."

Sadie groaned.

"Will I stay a little mite too?" asked Helen.

Riley scooped her up, squealing and laughing, onto his broad shoulder. "You're bigger than a mite already. If Sadie don't watch out, you'll shoot right over her and everybody will think you're the twelve-year-old."

Helen giggled harder and curled around Riley's head, but Sadie turned away with a flush. She hated being the runt of the family.

"Look at the tree York planted for me, Riley."

"It's a fine tree, Momma. I helped him get it. We rode out before the sun and got it from near the creek on the other side of his property line."

Momma's face lit up. "Were there more trees there?"

"Yes. Lots of trees. Maybe five or six."

"What kind?"

"Cottonwood."

"Any more oak?"

"I didn't notice."

"I like cottonwoods," said Web. "I like the pods that fly off them."

"And they each one have a fairy inside," said Helen. "I know. I opened some once. The fairies had flown away, but they left their little silk dresses behind."

"Just don't let them carry you off," said Riley, tickling Helen again until she sent peals of laughter over the silent prairie.

Momma shielded her eyes against the morning sun that was already bright and getting hot as she looked in the direction where Riley said they'd found the trees. "We're going to go get a few more trees just as soon as we're done with the garden, and we're going to plant some trees around this place and make it shady and beautiful."

"And flowers too, Momma," said Opal.

"Flowers and trees," said Momma, nodding and looking very determined.

Sadie knew when Momma talked like that, she meant just what she said.

Momma stopped just outside the soddy. "Don't say anything to York about us getting the trees or he'll feel he has to help. And he already has enough work for five men."

"Digging up a tree is hard work, Momma," Riley commented.

"It is," said Web, drooping in exaggeration as if he was bone-weary.

Momma lifted her rounded chin. "I've moved trees before. I know how to ball up the roots and how to plant them again. We can do it."

"Levi's coming today. Maybe he would help," said Opal.

Sadie scowled, but didn't say anything.

"He wouldn't know how," said Riley gruffly.

Opal turned on him. "How do you know? I bet he can do anything!"

"He can't plow."

"Let's finish breakfast, children."

Sadie walked inside the dark soddy. The smell of biscuits told her they were done, and she lifted the pan out of the oven and set it on a trivet on the table. Riley ran to the well to wash, and Opal flounced over to the stove to drop in a few buffalo chips.

The rest of the day Sadie didn't rest unless Momma said to, and then it was only for a short time. After York brought back Dick and Jane, he said he'd take a few biscuits and some beef jerky with him so he wouldn't have to come in for dinner. He'd said, "Pack enough for Levi. He's going to meet me near the windmill." Sadie saw the way Momma's thoughts leaped ahead to the time when they could go after the trees. With York gone until dark, they wouldn't have to be concerned about him learning what they had planned. And Momma wouldn't stop to fix a big noon dinner. They each ate a biscuit with molasses and drank milk kept cold in a jar hanging in the well.

When Riley finished plowing, while the others finished the last of the corn and potatoes Sadie helped him unload their belongings from the wagon, take off the heavy canvas cover, and spread it over the pile of stuff from the wagon. Riley hitched Dick and Jane, while Sadie found the heavy burlap bags and the bucket that Momma had said they'd need. From the soddy Riley took the rifle that once had been Pa's and laid it at his feet in the wagon.

"Tell Momma we're ready," he said as he pulled his hat low over his eyes.

Sadie cupped her hands around her mouth. "We're ready, Momma."

"Water Bossie, and we'll be right there," Momma called back.

Sadie carried a bucket of water to Bossie, moved her to a new grazing spot, then ran back to the yard.

Several minutes later Sadie sat beside Web on one side of the wagon, while Opal sat with Helen on the other side and Momma rode on the seat with Riley.

Opal had been very quiet all day, and Sadie knew it was because of her disappointment over not seeing Levi.

"It feels like we're going to a picnic, doesn't it?" asked Helen.

Web rubbed his stomach. "I wish I had some fried chicken right now. I'm starved."

Sadie's mouth watered, and she longed for a thick piece of dark meat, fried crisp on the outside but juicy on the inside. The biscuit with molasses she'd eaten for dinner at noon had not been enough.

"Remember the picnic we went on with Pa last Independence Day?" said Opal. "He told us a story about when he was a little boy in Pennsylvania."

Sadie turned her face to the wind and tried not to listen as the others laughed and talked about the good times with Pa.

At the creek Sadie jumped to the ground, while Dick and Jane drank noisily. She looked at the giant cottonwood that stood beside the water. The others climbed from the wagon too, and Web ran to the edge of the water and stuck in a toe.

"It's warm. Can I wade, Momma?"

"Yes."

"Me too?" asked Helen.

"Yes."

Web walked right in, laughing and calling for Helen to hurry, but she eased her way in until she stood ankle-deep beside him.

"Pollywogs!" cried Web.

"Let's catch 'em." Helen bent down with one hand in the water, the other holding her skirts up.

Sadie leaned against the cottonwood and watched the tiny leaves dance and twirl and flash with silver in the wind. She smelled the damp earth and occasionally felt a splash from Web or Helen. She heard Riley and Opal talking behind her, but paid no attention to what they were saying.

Momma walked along the narrow creek and caressed each tree. Finally she walked back. "All of them are too big for us to dig up. York got the only one small enough to handle."

She sounded so disappointed that Sadie wanted to reach out and comfort her, but Opal and Riley beat her to it.

Suddenly Dick whinnied and tossed his head. Sadie turned in time to see Jane shy away from Dick and whinny too. Their harness jangled.

Just then a rattlesnake whirred and Dick leaped forward, dragging Jane and the wagon with him.

"Whoa!" shouted Riley, running to head off the team. "Whoa, Dick! Jane, whoa!"

"Watch out for the snake!" shouted Momma. "Opal, come over here. Sadie, watch around you when you walk."

"Momma?" called Helen in a tiny voice.

"Stay in the water!" cried Sadie.

"Do!" said Momma.

Web awkwardly slipped an arm around Helen. "I'll take care of her."

Sadie watched the rattlesnake "taste" the area around it, then slither right toward her. She froze. It stopped, then eased past her just inches from her bare feet. When she was finally able to move, she walked over to stand beside Momma and Opal. For a long time nobody spoke.

"It's gone now, kids," Sadie said quietly. "You can come out now."

For a while no one said a word. Momma scanned the prairie, her forehead puckered slightly, watching for Riley. A frog croaked and splashed. Helen sneezed.

"Here he comes," whispered Sadie. She saw the defeated slump of his body as he half-ran, half-walked toward them.

Gasping for breath, his clothes soaked with

sweat, he stopped in front of Momma. "They got away."

"You did the best you could to catch them, Riley. We can't cry over spilt milk." Momma looked across the rolling hills and up at the sky that was already pink with sunset. "We'll run home. And we'll beat the team and York too."

Opal cleared her throat, but didn't voice the objection Sadie read on her face.

Sadie reached deep inside herself for all the strength she had left after such a long day. Momma had said they'd beat York and the team home, and she meant it.

7
Helen

With Web's hand tightly in hers, Sadie ran around the base of a small hill after Riley who carried Helen on his back. Opal and Momma followed close behind. A cloud passed over the late-afternoon sun, sending shadows across the prairie. Sadie could hear Web gasping for breath, and she slowed just a little. He was too big for any of them to carry, and if they'd tried he'd have been mortified. His greatest wish was to be as big and strong as Riley, and at times he was able to convince himself that he was.

Finally Sadie ran into the yard, where Riley and Helen were already drinking cold water from the well. Dick and Jane stood nearby, their heads down and the wagon safely behind them. York wasn't in sight.

Her legs trembling, Sadie sank beside Riley as he

offered her a dipper of water. She drank deeply, and the cold water slowly seeped through her dry throat and finally quenched her thirst. She dipped down for more and wanted to drink it, but handed it to Web instead, who grabbed it eagerly.

"We made it," said Momma, gasping for breath. She dropped to the ground, leaned against the wagon wheel, and pulled off her bonnet. Her face was red, and her chest heaved.

Opal dropped to the ground beside the well and waited for her turn with the tin dipper. She was flushed and disheveled and would've died first before she'd let any fine young man see her in such a state.

Web filled the dipper again and carried it to Momma. "Here, Momma."

"Thank you, Webster." She drained it, sighed, and handed it back to give to Opal.

Sadie walked to the shade of the wagon and sat beside Momma. "Riley and I will put the cover back on the wagon and load all the stuff back in."

Momma nodded. "Rest a bit first." She turned to Web. "While they load the wagon, you and Helen take the buckets and fill them with cow chips."

Sadie wiped her face with her apron and let the wind blow over her hot body and through her hair, which in the rush had come loose from its braids. She picked a cactus sliver from the bottom of her foot.

Momma reached for Helen's hand. "Did you remember to put the jug of milk down in the well?"

Sadie stiffened.

Helen leaned against Momma and looked at Sadie. "I didn't, but Sadie said she would."

Sadie jumped up. "I did not!" The lie stuck in her throat and hurt her right to the center of her heart. She didn't dare look at any of the others in case they could read her guilt. She knew they had to keep silent while Momma dealt with the problem.

Helen scrambled to her feet and looked at Momma and then Sadie and back again. "She did say she would, Momma."

Sadie put on her most innocent look. "No, Momma, I didn't." The look on Helen's face made Sadie almost tell the truth, but she quickly hardened her heart.

Momma slowly stood to her feet. In a stern voice she asked, "Helen, is the jug of milk in the well?"

All the color drained from Helen's face, and she trembled as she looked helplessly at Sadie.

"Don't ask me," said Sadie, looking right back at Helen.

Helen's wide blue eyes filled with tears, but she wouldn't let them fall. "It's not, Momma."

"Come here, Helen." Momma's voice was even angrier now, but her eyes were full of pain.

Helen took one step and then two, and she was close enough for Momma to touch her.

"Turn around, Helen."

Sadie wanted to run to the barn and hide in the darkest corner with Tanner.

Slowly Helen turned, her face set.

Sadie heard Opal suck in her breath. Riley cleared his throat. It had been a long time since Momma had had to spank any of them.

"Bend over."

Not a sound could be heard in all the vast prairie.

Helen bent over, and her tangled white hair swung forward to cover her cheeks.

Momma usually used a special spanking board that she kept on the window ledge, but this time she used her hand. She swatted Helen three times, and

Helen stood up. "You must learn to obey. You must never let good milk go to waste."

"I'm sorry," she whispered with her eyes downcast.

Sadie felt Helen's humiliation, but she couldn't—or wouldn't—speak up and tell the truth.

Momma turned to the others, and her voice was unsteady as she said, "Children, do your chores. Opal, milk Bossie and then help me fix supper."

Silently Sadie walked over to Riley to help put the bows in place and to stretch the cover over them. Heavy weights seemed tied to her feet and arms as she loaded the things back into the wagon.

Many times Pa had said to them when he'd heard of people who lied, "Lying is as bad as disobeying, and disobeying is as bad as stealing. Once you let sin in your life, it takes over. But that doesn't mean there's no way out. Jesus said that if we confess our sins to Him, He is faithful and just to forgive us our sins and to cleanse us from all unrighteousness."

She could see Pa sitting in his chair at the table when they had their daily Bible reading and prayer time. He'd talk about living holy lives, about loving others, about helping your neighbors, and about having a special friendship with God Himself.

A great yearning for the private prayer times she used to have welled up inside her. Then Pa's death flashed across her mind, and she knew she could never be close to God again. God could not possibly forgive her for what she'd done. She couldn't forgive herself either, and she never would.

Several minutes later Momma walked out of the soddy and looked around. "Where's Helen?"

Sadie looked at Riley, and he shrugged.

"We haven't seen her," he said.

"She went with Web," said Opal.

"I can see Web over there," said Momma, pointing to the lone speck in the prairie. "She must've come back."

Sadie looked toward Bossie, once again munching grass after Opal had milked her.

"Helen!" called Momma, raising her voice enough that it floated out over the prairie.

Opal stood at the edge of the field and called, "Helen!"

Sadie ran to the barn and burst through the barn door. The thick walls soaked up the light. "Helen. Helen, are you with Tanner?"

Tanner let out a feeble bark, but there was no answer from Helen. Sadie rested her hand on Tanner's head. "I've done a terrible thing," she whispered.

Tanner lifted his head and licked her hand. She wanted to be glad to see he was better, but her whole being was full of Helen.

Sadie raced out into the fading sunlight toward Web, standing beside Riley. Echoes of Helen's name filled the air.

"Have you seen Helen, Web?"

He frowned and wiped his arm across his hot face. "I told Riley she was helping me, but she said she wanted to get a surprise for Momma."

"And you let her go?"

"Don't, Sadie," said Riley with a frown.

Web just shrugged.

"How long ago was that?"

"A long time ago."

Sadie knew a long time to Web could be only a

few minutes, especially when he'd been working in the hot sun picking up chips. "How far did you go, Web?"

"Over that way around two hills." He pointed to the rolling hills this side of a taller hill.

"Tell Momma I'll find her."

"I'll go with you," said Riley.

"No!" She had to do it herself. "You look somewhere else." Sadie ran the way Web had pointed, her heart racing faster than her bare feet. Wind whipped her dress and apron against her legs. Wind whipped her hair into a frenzy. Wind whipped her bonnet against her back.

Once she almost stepped on a cactus, but she hop-jumped enough to miss it. A jackrabbit leaped high and bounced out of sight. Meadowlarks sang from where they swayed on timothy grass. Momma and Opal and Riley called Helen's name, but their calls faded away as Sadie ran.

She finally stopped at the base of the second hill, cupped her hands around her mouth and called urgently, "Helen!" She listened, but the only answer was the wind blowing the grasses that stretched forever around her.

With a heavy sigh she walked up the hill, making her way carefully in case the wind had whipped the top of the hill away, leaving a blowout. York had showed them blowouts on other hills. "The buffalo roamed here not long ago and tore up the grass, and the wind blew and blew and blew the sand away. Farther into the sandhills sometimes half a hill is blown away. I've heard tell that the wind made new hills with its blowing and blew down some others."

Sadie checked the hill, and it was solid. She stood at the crest and looked all around. She smelled the good soil and the sweet grasses. The sky full of puffy white clouds reached out and over and down and sat like a giant upside-down blue-and-white bowl over the prairie. York's cattle dotted one hillside. The soddies were dots the other way.

A shadow passed over her, and she looked up to see a red hawk. Her heart pounded, and she wondered if she looked small enough to the hawk to make a meal. When it flew out of sight, she breathed a sigh of relief.

"I'll walk to that hill and take a look." Her voice sounded strange in the stillness around her.

She ran down the hill and across the grass that reached almost to her knees. York said later in the spring the grass would be above her knees.

Just then the grass in front of her parted. She stopped and waited. A big bull snake slithered away, and the grass closed back again. She knew it wasn't poisonous, but she still didn't like to be near it. She ran toward the hill she'd marked with her eye and ran up it. She remembered York's warning and continued cautiously.

Abruptly she stopped. The top of the hill was gone, but the tall, waving grass around it had made it appear as if it was still there. She peeked down into the sandy hole, and there, curled up in a ball, was Helen.

Sadie dropped to her knees. "Helen!"

Helen lifted her head, then jumped up. Tears spilled down her face. "I called and called," she said. "I didn't think anybody would come."

"Climb out."

"I can't. Every time I try, I slide back down."

Sadie could see the marks in the sand where Helen had tried. "Don't be frightened. I'll get you out." If Helen were taller she could easily climb out, but she was short and couldn't grasp the roots of the tough grass at the rim of the blowout. Sadie didn't want to jump in because she might be too short as well. If she only had a rope, she could drop it down to Helen and help her climb out. Sadie wrinkled her brow in thought, then looked down at her apron. Quickly she untied it, lifted it over her head, and promised, "I'll get you out, Helen."

"I'm scared, Sadie."

"No need to be now."

"I thought you hated me."

"I don't."

"But you lied."

Sadie was quiet a long time. "I'm sorry," she admitted very softly.

"I won't tell Momma."

"Thank you." Sadie stretched out in the grass and held the apron by one end of the tie. The rest dangled down the sand into the blowout. "Take hold and climb up, Helen."

Helen stretched, but she couldn't quite reach. She ran up the side and touched the tie, but before she could get a grasp she slipped down the sand to fall at the bottom again.

"Try again, Helen! You can do it!" Sadie's mouth was bone-dry.

Helen took a deep breath, flapped her arms, screwed up her little face, and plowed as hard as she could up the side of the blowout. Her hand closed over the tie, held, then slipped off. She flopped back down and rolled to a stop. "Sadie, get me out! Please, Sadie!"

Sadie slowly pulled the apron up. "I'll get you out." An ant crawled across her leg, and she brushed it away. She touched the ties of the apron and wished she could somehow stretch them out to make them longer. An idea popped into her head, and her face lit up. "My bonnet!" She pulled off her bonnet, tied the string of the bonnet to the tie of the apron, tugged to make sure the knot would hold, then dropped it down to Helen.

Helen ran partway up the sand, grabbed the tie, and held on with both hands. The sudden weight almost jerked Sadie over the edge and into the blowout. She flattened out even more and dug her toes into the roots of the grass.

Inch by inch Helen crept up the blowout until she reached the rim. When she finally sprawled over the edge, Sadie pulled her close and held her tight to her heart.

"Thank you, Sadie! Thank you! You saved my life!"

Sadie smiled through her tears and held Helen tighter. Pa would be proud of her if he could see her now. But maybe in Heaven he could look down and watch what was going on. Maybe this very moment he was looking right through the big blue-white bowl and down on the grassy prairie at his daughters.

Please let him know, dear God, Sadie silently prayed. But don't let him know about the lies.

8

The Spy

Sadie crept around the base of the hill where Helen had been lost just a few days before. She knew Levi had brought Opal out to see the blowout, and Sadie wanted to spy on them. She didn't want Opal to tell Levi that he was a fine young man or, worse, that someday they could get married.

For some reason Sadie felt like Levi belonged to her—even though she was not thinking of marrying anyone now or even when she was sixteen. She'd never get married, but would stay near Pa's grave and tend it.

She saw Opal's pink-flowered sunbonnet, then her pink-flowered shoulders when Sadie suddenly dropped down. Her leg brushed a prickly pear, and she bit back a cry of pain. She pulled the cactus sticker out of her leg and rubbed it until it felt better. When she looked for Opal and Levi, they were out of sight again.

Meadowlarks sang all around her, filling the prairie with a glad song that struck Sadie to the heart. For just a moment she thought of turning back and not doing such a naughty thing as to spy, but then she crept forward until she heard their voices—Opal's gentle and almost as full of melody as the meadowlarks, and Levi's deep and pleasant.

Sadie strained to catch the words, but couldn't. So she quietly moved closer still. She saw them sitting next to each other on the side of the hill, and she stayed hidden around the bend.

A snake slithered through the sand, leaving its trail, but she didn't jump away because it was a garter snake and couldn't harm her. She inched closer, her face almost in the grass.

Finally she could hear Opal saying, "What a beautiful Sunday afternoon."

"I'm glad Paw said I could come to visit."

"Me too."

Sadie doubled her fists and gritted her teeth. When Levi had ridden up she'd thought he'd come to see her, but when his eyes had lit up at the sight of Opal she'd known better.

Opal laughed a gentle laugh. "I'm so glad we moved here, Levi. Is there a school nearby for us?"

"Jake's Crossing, but that's too far for me to go unless I moved to town."

"We can't go that far to school either. Momma will teach us again, I guess."

Opal sounded disappointed, and Sadie knew it was because Opal liked being around others. It didn't bother Sadie to go days on end without seeing another living soul except her family. Her mind was

always full of exciting things. Sometimes she longed
for paper to write them down, but there was never
paper for anything but letters to Momma's family in
Michigan. Momma had had Pa make slates for each of
them for their schoolwork. Sometimes Sadie had put
her thoughts down on the slate, but then she'd have to
rub them off to make room for lessons.

"Does your momma teach you?" Opal asked.

"No. Paw does." Something in Levi's voice made
Sadie think he had some secret he wasn't telling. She
wished she could find it out.

"That's wonderful that your pa finds the time."

"During the winter, after we check our traps, he
does."

"Pa used to trap."

Sadie thought of the times she'd trailed along
with Riley and Pa on icy cold mornings to check the
trap lines along the creek. Sometimes she'd have to
turn away at the sight of the beautiful animals caught
and dead, but then she'd remember that the pelts
paid for food and a plow and a harrow and shoes for
all of them.

"Your sister's a nice girl."

Sadie's ears pricked up.

"Which sister? I have two." Opal's voice was
crisp, and Sadie knew Opal didn't like Levi bringing
up any of her sisters.

"Sadie."

"Oh, yes. Sadie. She's a child."

"Aren't you?"

"Me? I'm fourteen!"

"And how old is Sadie?"

"Barely twelve."

"That was quite a tale about the way she saved
little Helen."

"Yes. She loved being a heroine."

Sadie flushed. She'd tried to keep Helen from telling the story, but Helen had told it over and over. York had held her on his lap and stroked her white hair that Momma had brushed until all the sand was out and listened every time she told it. He'd told Sadie that she deserved a big bear hug, and he'd promptly given her one. It had been hard for her to accept the attention.

"How old are you, Levi?"

"I'm sixteen."

Sadie wrinkled her nose at what was coming.

"I'm going to get married when I'm sixteen."

"Isn't that too young?"

"Young? Momma married Pa when she was sixteen and he was twenty-five. They settled a claim and raised a family. I will be old enough to marry at sixteen and to settle a claim with *my* husband."

"York says one of these days the rest of the sandhills will be open as free land, and when that time comes I'll get free land and raise cattle and horses just like York does. I want a big ranch, not a small one like Pa's. York said in Texas there are ranches as big as the whole state of Nebraska. I'd like to own a ranch that big."

"But that would mean you'd own the whole state of Nebraska unless you moved to Texas."

"I'd never move from Nebraska! Nebraska is my home!"

Sadie heard the pride in his voice, the same pride that she'd heard over and over all of her life. But then she'd heard anger and defeat too, from the people who had given up and moved away from the wind and the grasshoppers and the drought and the winter blizzards and the summer heat.

"I'd never move either, Levi. That is, unless my husband did."

Sadie rolled her eyes. A prickle of guilt for spying slipped over her, but she pushed it away.

"Does Sadie plan on getting married when she's sixteen?"

Sadie gasped, then clamped her hand over her mouth.

"Oh, Sadie! She never talks about getting married. She's such a . . . a child!"

They were silent a long time and then Levi said, "You glad your ma married York?"

"Yes."

"The schoolteacher in Jake's Crossing had her eye on York."

"She did?"

"But she won't have no trouble findin' a husband. There's other bachelors around here. Two live in a dugout over near our place. They staked claims side by side, and half the dugout is on one claim and the other half on the other. They're proving their claims and someday they say they'll build soddies, but for now they're happy."

"How old are they?"

"I don't know. Not as old as York, but older than me."

Sadie wanted to jump up and ask Opal if she could find something interesting to talk about, but she stayed hidden in the grass. A cottontail peeked around a hump of grass, then hopped away. An ant tickled her hand, and she shook it off.

"We were surprised, Paw and me, that York up and married. It was a bigger surprise that he married a widow with five kids. But a nice surprise."

"They met a couple of years ago when Pa bought

a horse from York while he was back east visiting. Then when York came again and Pa was . . . gone, he and Momma fell in love. It was very romantic."

Sadie wanted to throw up.

"They got married, sold our place, and we moved here."

"Did Sadie want to come?"

"I don't know!" Opal sounded very impatient.

"I see such a sadness in her eyes."

Sadie blinked.

"I think I'd better get back!" Opal announced in disgust.

Sadie could tell that Opal had jumped up to head home. Wildly Sadie looked around, then inched back farther around the hill. With her heart pounding she ran to a smaller hill and slipped around it, then ran again. If they climbed the hill and looked in her direction they'd see her! She ran around the base of another hill and suddenly swooshed down it just like on packed snow in the winter, except this time it was sand. She stopped at the bottom, picked herself up, and dusted herself off. She looked around at the emptiness stretching on and on and on. An uneasy feeling tugged at her.

"I'd better get back." Her voice was low, but it sounded loud in the silence around her.

She walked away from the blowout, careful to stay at the base of the rolling hills. She licked her dry lips, gritty with sand, and ran her tongue over her teeth and gums. They felt dry too—whether from the prairie or from the anxiety she felt, she wasn't sure.

She looked around, found a tall hill, and decided to climb it to get her bearings. Carefully she watched her step and when she reached the top, wind whipped against her, almost knocking her off her feet. She shielded her eyes with her hand and looked in every direction. She couldn't see dots of cattle or dots of trees or dots of soddies.

Fear shook her and dampened her palms with perspiration. But then she saw a rider come around the base of her hill. Her heart leaped and she shouted through cupped hands, "Wait! I need to talk to you!"

She ran down the hill, her arms spinning like windmills to keep her from falling.

The rider waited for her, and she saw that it was an old man on a mule. Just a few feet away from him, she stopped and stared. She saw the long salt-and-pepper beard and the rough, dirty clothes and boots the color of polished copper. She saw the rifle lying easily across his lap and the lariat looped over the saddle horn. Ty Bailer looked right at home on the back of his brown mule in the middle of the prairie.

"I been watchin' ya," he said in a terrible voice.

She wanted to turn and run, but she had the feeling that if she did he'd catch her in a minute.

"I . . . I have to go home."

"I been watchin' ya watch the Cass boy and his girl."

Sadie's heart dropped to her feet. He'd been spying on her while she spied on Opal and Levi!

"I wanted to get the Cass boy as well as you, prairie chicken, but he walked with the girl back to York's place, and you came off by yerself, and so I said to myself that I just as leave grab you when the opportunity presented itself."

Suddenly she turned and fled from the man and the mule and the wicked laugh that pursued her.

Something struck her arm, and she glanced back to see a loop at her side. He was trying to rope her! She ran harder, dust puffing up from her feet. Today she wore shoes because it was Sunday and because company had come.

Every second she expected to feel the rough sting of the rope, and then it came so fast that it jerked her off her feet and sent her flying backward to land with a thud on her rump.

9

Ty Bailer

For a minute everything was dark, and then light—and pain—burst over her and she struggled to stand, only to have the rope tighten and jerk her off her feet again. Sand gritted in her teeth and pressed into her legs and filled her shoes.

The old man sat on his mule and looked down at her, his face dark with anger. "Ya can't fool around with Tyler Bailer and get by with it, ya runt of a girl!"

She struggled harder, and the rope scratched her arms and dug through her dress and pinched her waist. Her ears buzzed, and she thought for a minute the darkness would close over her again. But her head cleared, and the man and the long-eared brown mule and the prairie stood in crisp focus before her. "Let me go," she gasped.

He looped his end of the rope to the saddle horn, slid off the mule and said, "Stand and hold, Jasmine."

Sadie eyed the man, weighing the situation as she slowly stood to her feet. She took a step forward to ease the rope enough to slip it off. But as the rope slackened, the mule backed up just enough to make it taut again. She took a step forward, and the sleepy-eyed mule took a step back. She looked at the mule and frowned. Carefully she inched forward and casually started to loosen the loop. Jasmine took a step back. Sadie shook her head in amazement. She'd never seen such a thing before.

Suddenly she yelled and ran forward, but Jasmine backed up just as fast and jerked her off her feet. She fell with a thud and just lay there, aching all over.

"I told ya you'd pay for makin' me a laughin' stock, prairie chicken." He grinned, and she saw the tobacco stain on his chipped teeth, on his lip, and down his salt-and-pepper beard.

The mule brayed, and Ty Bailer said, "You tell her, Jasmine!"

He followed the rope right to Sadie's waist.

She smelled the tobacco on his breath and the sweat on his clothes, and she turned her head away.

"Now we'll see how much fight ya have in ya."

"Let me go," she whispered.

"Let ya go? When snow flies in July." He spit a stream of tobacco that landed in a brown, ugly mass on an anthill near her foot. He rubbed the back of a grubby hand across his mouth and narrowed his eyes into slits. "Ya don't look so feisty now, ya little bit of nothin'."

"What are you going to do with me?" She

squirmed, but the rope bit into her and she stopped before her arms bled.

"Yer comin' with me, prairie chicken." He yanked her to Jasmine and with great ease lifted her up into the saddle, then mounted behind her and put both filthy arms around her to grab the reins.

She stared down at his thin arms covered with a red plaid shirt that looked as if it hadn't ever been washed and his narrow hands that looked like old shoe leather. A bitter taste filled her mouth. "Let me go!"

"I'll let ya go." He chuckled deep inside his narrow chest. "Jest as soon as we're shed of this place."

Fear gripped her, and the world around her spun. She thought she was going to pass out. She forced back the weakness and struggled for the strength that she knew she'd need to survive. He was going to let her go when they were far out on the prairie away from York's homestead, away from Jake's Crossing, and maybe out into the Great North American Desert that was only fit for coyotes and wild cattle.

She gripped Jasmine with her knees so that she wouldn't have to depend on the arms on either side of her to keep her in the saddle. "York will trail us and find me."

"If he tries, I'll shoot him."

She saw the gun in the boot beside her leg, and she trembled. Was she going to be the cause of York's death just as she was for Pa's? Scalding tears burned the backs of her eyes, but she wouldn't let them fall where Ty Bailer could see. He'd never make her cry, never turn her into a whimpering baby.

She sat with her back stiff, her chin up as the

mule picked its way around the small hills that she knew were taking her farther and farther from York's place. On her left the sun rested on the top of a hill, grew bigger and bigger, and slowly slipped behind it to leave a blaze of glory behind.

"I see the pup didn't die."

She trembled at the thought of him spying on her. "No, he didn't die and he won't die."

"He's a no-account mutt."

She snapped her mouth closed.

"I'll kill him yet."

She bit her lower lip until she tasted blood.

"And it'll give me great pleasure."

Still she said nothing.

He stopped talking, and the creak of the leather and his breathing and the sounds of the wind around her flooded her mind until she wanted to scream.

Long shadows lay over the prairie now. A bird called. The wind changed and turned cool against Sadie's skin.

When a strange snorting noise covered the other sounds, slowly, carefully Sadie turned her head until she could see Ty Bailer. His head had dropped on his chest, and his mouth had dropped open. He'd fallen asleep. Tobacco juice ran from the corner of his mouth and down into his salt-and-pepper beard. She turned quickly away.

Her heart raced. Slowly, carefully she loosened the rope around her and cautiously eased it over her head. She pulled the reins from Ty Bailer's hands, then twisted around and shoved Ty with all of her strength. He slid off Jasmine and landed with a grunt.

Cursing, he leaped up and grabbed for Jasmine and Sadie.

Sadie shouted to Jasmine, slapped her with the

reins, and kicked her sides. Jasmine brayed and jumped forward and then stretched out in a run, her long ears back. Sadie clung to the saddle horn and the reins, with Ty's yells echoing behind her.

When she felt a safe distance from Ty, she pulled back on the reins to stop Jasmine—only to discover that she wouldn't stop. Sadie pulled harder. "Whoa! Whoa, Jasmine!" Wind threw the words across the prairie and whipped her face and her clothes and her sunbonnet.

Jasmine ran until her sides heaved, until her mouth and coat were foamy.

Suddenly she stopped, her front legs stretched out ahead of her and her head down. Sadie flew over the saddle and over Jasmine's head and landed with a jarring thud. Jasmine brayed, kicked her heels, and raced back the way she'd come.

Sadie moaned and carefully sat up. The rolling hills and bright sky spun, and she closed her eyes and moaned again. When she opened her eyes, the world stood still. Slowly she stood and rubbed her back and brushed sand off her legs and skirt.

The red sky faded to pink, and she knew it would change again and again until it was gray, and then the gray would darken to night.

A pack of coyotes yip-yipped, and she watched them run across a flat area. There were seven of them and they looked like thin dogs with pointed ears, light yellow coats, and long tails that floated behind them. She stood still, her eyes wide and her mouth dry. York had said coyotes wouldn't bother humans, but she wondered if the coyotes knew that. They ran out of sight, and she breathed easier.

Slowly she walked forward, then stopped. She was lost and she knew it. She remembered Momma and York talking about the size of Nebraska while they sat around the campfire on their trip from Douglas County.

Momma had said, "Nebraska is so big that all the New England states and most of New York State could fit into it. But of course it's not as big as Texas."

"No state is as big as Texas. And none ever will be," York stated proudly.

Sadie looked all around her. She could walk for days and still be in Nebraska. "I'll climb a hill and see what I can see." Her voice broke, and she swallowed hard.

A few minutes later she reached the top of a hill and looked all around. As far as she could see there were no homes or people or cattle or windmills. All she could see was shadowed prairie and a giant darkening sky.

A whimper rose in her throat and escaped before she could stop it. "Which way is home?" she asked the prairie softly.

Her mind whirled, and she couldn't think straight. She looked up toward Heaven and whispered, "Please, God, help me. I know I'm bad for spying on Opal and Levi, and I'm bad for lying, and I'm even worse for making Pa die in the blizzard, but please help me anyway. Momma says You love me, and Momma doesn't lie."

She stood and waited, but no voice boomed down from Heaven to tell her directions.

"I'll try south," she said finally, and felt better. She walked south, and the sky darkened more and night fell. Stars flashed and twinkled and seemed close enough to touch. She thought she could pluck them out of the sky if she stood on tiptoe on one of the tall hills. A whippoorwill called, and coyotes howled.

Could she survive all night on the prairie by herself?

Cold wind beat against her, and her feet ached.

She walked, careful of every step she took.

She saw a star low to the ground and followed it, startled that it stayed low to the ground even when she got closer.

A dog barked.

She stopped, her hand on her racing heart.

Was it Tanner?

"Hello!"

The dog barked harder. The star bobbed, and she realized it was a light.

"Help me!"

"Who's out there? Speak up or I'll shoot!"

Sadie trembled. "It's Sadie Rose Merrill." She'd forgotten that it was no longer Merrill but York. "I'm lost."

The light bobbed closer. "No, you're not lost."

"I *am* lost!"

"You're here, ain't ya? Yer not lost atall."

Sadie finally made out the figure of a tall woman carrying a lantern. A big dog walked at her side.

"How'd you get out here all by yer lonesome?"

Sadie struggled with the tears that threatened to fall. "A man grabbed me and carried me off and I got away." The tears sounded in her voice, but there was nothing she could do about that.

"I'll be switched. What man? He got a name?"

"Ty Bailer."

"Heard tell he was ornerier than a sidewinder, but never laid eyes on him."

"He's ornery, all right." Sadie wanted to grab the woman's hand and cling to it, but she stayed with her hands at her sides.

"Sadie, you say."

"Yes."

"I'm Jewel Comstock. Call me Jewel. Everybody does."

"Jewel."

"My dog's Malachi. From the Bible."

"Hello, Malachi."

The dog lifted its paw to Sadie, and she took it and suddenly felt a little better.

"I have a dog. Tanner. I took him away from Ty Bailer because he was going to kill him."

"Whew!" Jewel laughed, and the lantern bobbed in her hand. "That's one story I want to hear, but not 'til morning. Sadie girl, you come home with me and get a good night's rest. Then we'll have us a good heart-to-heart in the morning."

Sadie weakly followed the woman and the dog across the empty prairie.

10

The Homesteader

Sadie stumbled along beside Jewel Comstock and Malachi to the greater darkness ahead. At each step the lantern lit enough of the way to see where she was going. Finally she saw the front door of the woman's house. It was tucked into the side of the hill with the front made of sod.

Inside, Jewel hung her rifle above the door, lit the lamp on the wooden table, and blew out the lantern. Fumes and smoke rose. The lamp cast a small glow over a section of the room. The walls were white, not dark and gloomy like York's soddy. The room felt snug and warm and didn't seem at all like a dugout.

Sadie sank weakly to a wooden chair and leaned her aching head against the fancy carving. She noticed another chair like it across the table. A Bible and a pair of spectacles lay on the table beside a small basket with a white cloth over it.

The woman pulled off her wide-brimmed hat, tossed it on a peg near the door, and handed Sadie a dipper of water. She drank thankfully with Malachi watching her with his bright eyes, black as buttons. When she handed the dipper back, the woman dipped a dipper for the dog and poured it in a bowl at the base of the washstand.

Jewel turned and stood with her hands on her wide hips. She was tall and big-boned and had a nose like a hook. "I don't recollect any Merrills livin' around here."

Sadie shook her head. "We're Merrills, but Momma married York and so we're York now, not Merrill. I forgot for a while."

"York." The woman nodded and grinned. "Now, that's a man. I'd married him myself if I'd been a few years younger. Or him a dozen or so years older. Or if I'd been handsome like I was when I was young. I *was* handsome when I was young. Except for my nose, of course."

Sadie couldn't think of anything nice to say about Jewel's nose, so she didn't say anything.

Jewel nodded. "He knows how to work, that York does. Funny thing about havin' only one name like that. You'd think if a man was goin' to name a little orphan baby, he'd do him right and give him two names."

Sadie could tell Jewel expected a response. "It is strange."

"He's not much of a sod-buster, but he knows ranchin' and ranchin' is what's goin' to make this part of Nebraska come to life." She talked about the soil and the wild hay that had fed buffalo for years and the water just under the ground in places. "Windmills have made it possible to run more cattle here. I have me a windmill, and I like to hear the squawk it makes and see the water gush out of the pipe into the tank."

Sadie wanted to interrupt the woman and ask how far from home she was, but she knew she must never interrupt an adult.

"You hungry?"

Sadie nodded. "But I could wait and eat when I get home."

"That won't be till morning. You bed down here tonight, and I'll take you home after chores." The woman pulled an apron over her faded dress. "In case you forgot, my name's Jewel Comstock. Quite a handle to put on me, but I was pretty in my heyday." She smiled and dropped a cow chip into the stove. "I was born in Bellevue, so I'm a native Nebraskan. I'm the only one in these parts."

"I was born in Nebraska."

Jewel jerked up as if she'd been hit. "You don't say."

"My brothers and sisters too."

"You don't say!"

"Riley's sixteen, Opal fourteen, me—I'm Sadie—twelve, Webster nine, and Helen eight. There's five of us, and we were born on a homestead in Douglas County."

"You don't say." Jewel leaned weakly against the wall beside the stove.

Sadie could see Jewel set a lot of store in being the only Nebraska-born person around, and she searched her mind to help her new friend feel her pride again. Finally she said, "But we never had to fight Indians like you most likely did. And we weren't born in the oldest town in Nebraska like you."

Jewel nodded and stood tall and once again worked at the stove, frying leftover cornmeal mush in a heavy skillet. She handed Sadie the plate of fried mush and pulled a biscuit out of a basket on the table.

"I could give you a cup of coffee."

"No thanks. But why don't you have one while I eat?"

"I'll do that." Jewel looked in the container of coffee beans, sighed, and closed it. "Best save it for morning. It'll be a while before I get to town again." She sat down across from Sadie, and Malachi turned around twice and settled at her feet. "I will have a biscuit." She opened the white cloth in the basket and took out two, gave one to Malachi and took a bite of hers.

"The mush was good, but I'm sorry I put you to such bother," said Sadie.

"No trouble. It's good to have you here. It's been a long time since I saw another human."

"Oh?"

Jewel pushed back stray straggles of gray hair and secured it in the bun at the nape of her skinny long neck. "Since March second. Yes, March second. It was the day before the blizzard that kept me snowed in for a week."

Sadie couldn't imagine how it would be not to see or talk to another person for over a month.

"I'm glad I have Malachi."

Malachi lifted his great head and slapped his cord of a tail on the packed dirt floor.

"We had a dog at home," said Sadie. "Pa's dog Racer. He's only a mutt, but he obeyed Pa better than we did, Pa always said. And we had to obey him."

"As you should. Children these days are spoiled. I even heard a boy in town sass his ma. I wanted to give him a piece of my mind, but I bit my tongue and didn't."

"I have Tanner now. That's the dog Ty Bailer was goin' to kill."

"Let's hear that story." Jewel leaned back and crossed her arms over her chest. "Don't leave out a single detail. I'm hungry for talk."

Sadie told the story and ended with how she'd escaped from Ty and wandered around lost. She hurried over the part about spying on Opal and Levi, but Jewel didn't miss a thing.

"You and your sister, do you get along?"

"Most of the time."

"I had a sister, but she died when I was five, so I don't remember much about her. Mildred was her name. I had me a baby too when my man and me first moved west. He died. John, I named him, after my papa." Jewel blinked and cleared her throat. The fire crackled. From outdoors an owl hooted. "My man, Eli, died not long after, and I've been on my own ever since. I had me a dog named Butch. When he died about seven years ago, I got Malachi. We've been through thick an' thin, old Malachi and me have."

Each time his name was mentioned, Malachi slapped the floor with his tail.

Warmth from the stove, the trying day, and Jewel's voice made Sadie droop with fatigue. Her eyelids closed, and she forced them open. Jewel's voice faded and grew loud and faded again.

Once she felt herself being picked up, and she remembered the times Pa had carried her to bed when she was young. She felt her shoes come off and then her stockings, and her feet could breathe, and then she didn't know anything until she sat up.

"It's morning!" Already the sun was up and birds

were talking to each other. The smell of coffee and pancakes filled the room. She looked at the pallet she'd slept on and saw that her dress and apron lay beside it with her shoes and stockings. She'd slept in her underwear. Her apron was torn, and she knew she'd have to patch it when she got home. She slipped the dress over her head and buttoned the buttons up the back, stretching and squirming to reach the ones in the center of her back. She ran her fingers through her hair and knew it would have to do until she got home to her brush.

The door opened, and Jewel walked in with Malachi at her heels. She wore the same faded dress as yesterday and the battered broad-brimmed hat. The men's shoes she had on made her feet look extra large.

Sadie stepped forward. "I want to help with chores."

"Not necessary. I saw you sleepin' sound as a baby, and I didn't have the heart to wake you." Jewel walked to the stove, lifted the pot, and poured a cup of thick, black coffee into a tin cup. She held it out to Sadie. "Want a cup?"

"No, thank you."

"Pancakes are staying warm in the oven. Take a trip to the outhouse if you want. It's just this side of the barn. Can't miss it."

Sadie ran outdoors into the bright, fresh morning and looked around. A creek gurgled a few feet away down a little path. Two giant cottonwoods and several small ones lined it, their leaves twirling and dancing in the wind. A sod barn and the outhouse stood to her left. A cow bawled, and a horse nickered. Birds sang as if their throats would burst. It was a beautiful day and she was alive and soon she'd be back with her family! She laughed, and the sound joined the melodies of the birds and the music of the creek.

Later Jewel hitched her team to the wagon, and Sadie stood with her mouth hanging open. Jewel's team was a brown cow with wide horns and a small gray horse with white mane and tail just bigger than pony size. The cow stood quietly and chewed her cud. The horse stamped impatiently and swished its white tail.

"Everybody stares the first time," Jewel said with a chuckle. "You get used to 'em. Annie and Ernie, my team. Annie's the cow. Ernie's the gelding."

"They are . . . nice. Different." Sadie giggled. "Nice."

"That they are." Jewel laughed a great laugh, and Sadie didn't feel so bad about giggling.

She climbed up the wheel and into the wagon to sit on the seat beside Jewel. Malachi stood on the ground on Jewel's side of the wagon, watching her as if to catch every word she said and every movement she made. A crate sat in the back with a white setting hen on a nest. She clucked and settled closer to her nest, her feathers fanned out and her beady eyes looking through the slats. Her bright red comb bobbed.

"Thought your ma might like chickens. Eggs'll hatch any day now."

Sadie's dark eyes sparkled as she smiled. "Why, thank you, Jewel!"

Jewel beamed as she slapped the reins on the horse and cow and clicked her tongue for them to "gittap."

The wagon lurched forward, and Sadie grabbed the seat and spread her feet for balance.

After a long time Jewel said, "Your ma's probably worried."

"Yes."

"York's probably searchin' high and low for you."

Sadie hung her head, and her sunbonnet blocked her face. How she hated to cause trouble for anyone!

"I bet old Ty'll hightail it out of the state. He won't want to face York after what he done."

Wide-eyed, Sadie turned to face Jewel. "What *will* York do?"

"Hunt Ty Bailer down most likely."

"Oh!"

"York's not one to sit back and let his family be walked over. From his talk about wanting a family to call his own, I know he values a family highly. Especially since he never had one before."

Sadie hadn't thought about York going after Ty Bailer. "I don't want York to get hurt."

"York's tough as nails. He was raised in the saddle with a gun in one hand and a rope in the other."

Sadie bit her lip. "Will he . . . shoot Ty Bailer?"

"He don't go in for killin' being as how he's a Christian man and don't believe in takin' a life, but he'll see that Ty Bailer can't stay in these parts."

Would York hunt Ty Bailer down because of her?

She could hear him say, "And I have enough love in my heart for you, Sadie Rose." The words worked their way around her heart and sent warmth through it, and then she remembered Pa and her heart froze over again.

The wagon bumped and rocked while Jewel talked nonstop all the way to York's place.

"Thanks for bringin' me home, Jewel," said Sadie.

"Us Nebraska natives got to stick together." Jewel winked and then turned to greet the family as they burst from the soddy.

Sadie dropped to the ground and faced Momma.

"Sadie," Momma whispered. She wrapped her arms around Sadie and held her close.

"I'm safe, Momma. I'm safe," Sadie said into the sweet smell of Momma's shoulder.

11

A Talk with Momma

Sadie held tighter to Momma. She had so much she wanted to say, but nothing came out.

"What's the signal for York to say the girl's been found?" asked Jewel.

"Two rifle shots," said Momma over Sadie's shoulder.

Jewel shot twice into the air, and Sadie jumped. Jewel dropped to the ground beside her wagon and rested her hand lightly on Malachi's head.

"Momma, this is Jewel Comstock. She found me and let me stay with her last night. Jewel, my momma, Bess York."

"Glad to meet you, Bess," said Jewel, shaking Momma's hand like a pump handle. "Your Sadie girl is a precious one."

"Thank you."

Helen looked up at Jewel. "Do you know you have a cow hooked to your wagon?"

Momma saw the team and said, "Oh, my."

Sadie noticed Opal and Web looking at the team, and she chuckled as she introduced Jewel to them.

Jewel said, "I once had a regular team, but my mare Glory up and died on me, and all I had was my Annie. So I trained her to pull with Ernie. Annie and Ernie don't know they look funny together, so I never tell them."

"I'll water them," said Web.

"I brought you a laying hen, Bess," said Jewel, lifting the crate from the back of the wagon.

"That's wonderful!" Momma's eyes twinkled. "I've wanted chickens. Thank you!" She looked at it and stuck her finger too close and the hen pecked her, but Momma didn't seem to mind.

"Girls, take the hen to the barn and find her a safe place to nest."

Jewel patted the crate. "You keep her in the crate a few days. I'll get it back from you when I'm in these parts—or if you come my way, drop it off."

"Thank you. Come inside and we'll talk."

Sadie watched them walk away. Jewel's big shoes made big puffs of dust, and Malachi padded along close behind. Momma barely reached Jewel's shoulder.

Opal touched Sadie's arm. "I'm glad you're back. I was so scared!"

"You were?"

Opal nodded as she tugged at her faded and patched blue dress that she always wore on wash day. She looked as if she hadn't slept well. "We all were afraid for you."

"How did you get lost?" asked Helen curiously as she followed them and the hen to the barn.

"I'll tell you all about it," said Sadie. They set the crate in the barn, and she talked to Tanner while her mind raced on what she should say to keep from telling Opal that she'd spied on her.

"We took good care of Tanner for you," said Helen.

"Thank you."

"He stood up," said Helen. "I think he was looking for you."

"Were you, Tanner?" Sadie hugged him and noticed the last of the matted hair was gone. "You brushed him clean."

Helen smiled and nodded. "Web and me did it."

"Thank you." A lump filled her throat.

"Were you scared?" asked Opal.

"Yes." Sadie patted Tanner, and he followed her a few steps and then sank down with his head on his front legs.

With the girls beside her, Sadie walked to the shade of the house and sat down on the grass. "We'll wait for Web so I don't have to tell the story again." That would also give her more time to decide just how to start the story.

"Hurry up, Web," called Helen.

Web led the team to the barn and then ran back and dropped down in front of Sadie. He wore bib overalls that were too short, but his hair was combed neatly. Sadie was glad she'd cut his hair Saturday. She smiled at Web, then looked at Helen on one side of her and Opal the other.

"Did Indians get you?" asked Web.

"No. Ty Bailer."

Web whistled, and the girls gasped.

"I was out in the prairie, and he'd been spying on me to get even with me because of Tanner." She breathed a sigh of relief over the slick way she'd gotten past her own spying. With many interruptions from the others, she told her story in great detail. She ended with, "And I was never so glad to see anyone in all my life as I was to see Jewel Comstock and her dog."

Hoofbeats pounded on the ground, and Sadie looked up to see York riding hard toward her. He leaned low over Bay's neck as wind whipped the loose part of his shirt. Bay stopped short three feet away, and York leaped to the ground and scooped Sadie up in his arms all in one easy movement.

She felt his heart thud against her and smelled the sweat of his shirt.

"Sadie Rose. Sadie Rose. I thought I'd lost you."

She could hear tears in his voice, and tears sprang to her eyes, and she couldn't blink them away no matter how hard she tried. Sobs shook her body, and she clung to York and didn't want to let him go.

Finally he held her away from him, wiped away her tears with his big bandanna, kissed both her cheeks, and said, "Now suppose you tell me where you've been."

Once again she sat down on the grass with her audience around her and she told the story again, this time with help from the girls and Web. Sadie saw anger flare in York's face when she told about Ty Bailer. He smiled when she told about Jewel and Malachi.

"Is Jewel in the house?" asked York when she finished.

"Yes. She sure does like you."

York grinned. "She's one fine homesteader. She saved my life a couple of times when I was wintering cattle here for the Texas Box W. I'll go thank her for saving yours." He strode to the house and called over his shoulder, "Web, take care of Bay for me please."

Web led Bay to be watered and then to the barn to unsaddle her just as Riley rode in.

"Now we can hear the story again," said Helen, pumping Sadie's arm up and down.

"I'll take care of Jane so Riley can listen to you," said Opal.

Riley handed her the reins an dropped beside Sadie. "I told Momma you were too tough for anything bad to happen to you."

Sadie laughed.

"But bad things did happen to her," said Helen. "Tell him, Sadie."

And so she did. Her mouth felt dry from talking so much. And as long as she didn't let herself think about it, she didn't feel guilty about spying on Opal and Levi.

"I'd like to get my hands on Ty Bailer!" Riley slammed his right fist into his left palm, making a loud pop. He scanned the prairie with narrowed eyes. "I wonder where he is right now."

Sadie shivered and looked out into the prairie. "He said he'd kill Tanner. He said he would, and I believe him."

"We'll let Tanner sleep in the wagon with us," said Riley.

"And in the daytime I'll watch him," said Helen.

Later, after Jewel had ridden away, Momma took Sadie aside, telling the others that she wanted to

speak to her alone. Sadie's heart raced, and for a
minute she wanted to call Jewel back and ask to go
home with her.

Momma sat down in the shade beside the house
near the tree. She looked serious, and Sadie wanted
to run. "Jewel told me what happened."

Sadie bit her lip. Jewel wouldn't have left out the
spying part.

"Sadie, I am very sorry for what happened to
you. I was afraid . . . I'd never see you again. Only
when I prayed did I have peace." She took Sadie's
hand and pressed her soft cheek to it. "You have always been very obedient, Sadie, and never made trouble. But I've felt a difference in you ever since your
pa . . . died. We were all sad about the accident and
we all missed him, still miss him, but we know we
must get on with life. But you don't seem to be able
to. Why not, Sadie?"

"I don't know." Couldn't Momma remember that
Pa's death had been her fault?

"Is it because of York?"

Sadie shook her head.

"Your pa was a hard-working man, and he didn't
have much time for play, but he was a fair man and he
loved all of us very much. He loved *you* very much.
He wouldn't want any of us to suffer because of him,
and especially when we know he's having a wonderful
time in Heaven with Jesus. Pa would say, what's done
is done—get on with livin'."

"Momma, I want to go back to live with Emma.
Please. It would be better for all of us."

Momma stiffened, and pain flashed in her eyes.
"Why would you want to go live with her?"

"She's my friend."

"We're your family."

"I miss her. And if I'm there with her I can tend Pa's grave."

"He wouldn't want you worrying over his grave or his body any more than he'd want you to worry over his work shirt. His body was only a jacket that covered the real man. He left the jacket behind and went to live in Heaven where he won't have to break sod or harvest crops or fight grasshoppers."

Why didn't Momma say, "His death wasn't your fault, Sadie, so stop blaming yourself." Sadie gave her a chance to say it, but she knew Momma couldn't because deep in her heart she did blame her and she'd blame her forever. With her heart heavy Sadie said, "I didn't want him to die."

"None of us did."

"How can you love York?"

"I just can."

"Did you quit loving Pa?"

"I still love him, but it's different now that he's gone. I love York, and I need him. So do you children."

Sadie fingered her sunbonnet string.

Momma moved her legs and brushed an ant off her finger. "Sadie, you know it was wrong to spy on Opal and Levi."

Sadie hung her head, and her cheeks burned.

"I won't spank you because you have already had a great deal of punishment because of your actions. You had a dreadful time, and that's trouble enough. But you must not spy any more. And you will stay close to the yard in case that dreadful man tries for you again."

"Yes, Momma." Sadie glanced sideways to see

Helen watching and listening to them. Sadie frowned, and Helen ducked out of sight at the corner of the house.

"And you must apologize to Opal."

"But, Momma, she doesn't know I spied on her."

"You must."

"Yes, Momma."

She stood up and shook down her skirts. "Help Opal finish the washing."

Sadie walked across the yard toward the washstand where Opal was scrubbing Riley's shirt up and down on the washboard.

Helen ran to Sadie. "I heard what you did. You spied on Levi and Opal!"

Sadie stopped short and glared down at Helen. "Don't you dare tell!"

"I won't. But you have to." Helen ran to Opal. "Sadie has something to tell you. And you won't like it."

Opal lifted a fine brow. "Oh?"

Sadie pushed Helen aside. "Momma just said to make sure you get the stains out."

Helen's mouth made a big "O," and she tugged on Sadie's arm.

"Leave me alone, Helen."

"But, Sadie . . ."

She pushed her face down close to Helen's. "If you ever want to touch Tanner again, you leave me alone."

12
The Lie

Sadie rested against the hoe and looked over at the clothes stretched out to dry on the sweet prairie grass. She knew she should feel wonderful because she was home and her family loved her and the washing was finished and she was almost done hoeing the tiny weeds in the garden. And yet she felt sick right to her heart. Her stomach was balled in an icy knot. Hot tears lurked at the backs of her eyes, and she knew they'd fall for no good reason when she least expected it.

As she stood there, she saw Helen playing with the huge toad she'd found. The toad hopped close to the still-wet clean clothes and then hopped right across the still-wet clean clothes—and Helen followed, laughing and squealing.

Sadie gulped.

Helen suddenly stopped, looked down, then looked around to see if anyone had seen her. She didn't notice Sadie.

"That bad girl," muttered Sadie.

Helen jumped off the clothes, caught her toad, and ran away to play somewhere else.

Sadie dropped the hoe and ran out of the garden, shouting, "Helen! Come here right now, Helen!" The wind caught the words and carried them along.

Helen didn't come, so Sadie stopped close to Momma's tree and called again.

Finally Helen walked around the house and said, "Were you callin' me, Sadie?"

"You know I was!" Sadie shook her finger at Helen. "You got all the clean clothes dirty! Just look at them! See all that extra work you made for us?"

Helen cringed, and her face turned whiter than the sheets that Momma had washed herself.

"You march right out there, get those clothes, and bring them to me."

"I won't!"

"You're going to wash them yourself."

"I won't!"

Sadie grabbed Helen and spanked her hard across the bottom just as Momma walked out of the soddy with a scowl on her face.

"What are you shouting about, Sadie? What are you doing?"

"She spanked me, Momma," Helen said in her saddest voice.

Sadie pointed at Helen. "*She* just got all the wash dirty!"

Helen's eyes widened. "I did not!"

Sadie's mouth fell open. Helen had never lied in her life. "Don't you dare tell a lie, Helen York!"

"Stop that!" Momma's voice rang out. "Shame on you, Sadie. Don't call your sister a liar. And don't you ever spank her."

Sadie sputtered until she could finally speak. "But she did lie! She got all the clean clothes dirty with her toad and her feet!"

Helen stood with an innocent look on her face and shook her head. "No, Momma. I was playing over there with my toad, and I did not get the clothes dirty. But I saw some kind of big animal run across them."

Momma turned to Opal, who had just walked up. "Did you see what happened?"

"I saw Helen over there, but she wasn't near the clothes."

Sadie's heart hammered, and she wanted to scream at the top of her lungs.

Momma turned to Web. "Web?"

"I don't know anything. I was with Tanner in the barn."

"Momma, she walked on the clothes!" cried Sadie. "I saw her with my own two eyes. Big as day she walked on the clothes!"

Momma was silent a long time, and then she said in a soft voice, "Helen, go into the house and get my spanking board off the window ledge and bring it to me."

Helen trembled as she walked slowly to the house.

Sadie smiled and relaxed. The warm, gentle wind tugged at her skirts.

Momma stood quietly, her arms crossed, and waited for the spanking board. No one made a sound. Finally Helen walked out with the board and slowly held it out. Momma took it and Helen turned around, big tears on her little ashen cheeks.

"Sadie, come here," said Momma.

Sadie froze.

"Sadie . . ." said Momma in a quiet, frightening voice.

Helen slowly turned and looked from Momma to Sadie. Opal reached out and pulled Helen to her side. Web stepped closer to Opal.

Sadie looked at Momma's face and at the board in her hand. She wouldn't look at the others who were witnessing her great disgrace.

"Turn around, Sadie."

Sadie gasped. She hadn't been spanked since she was ten years old—she was much too old to be spanked.

"Turn around, Sadie."

Slowly she turned, her toes biting into the ground.

"Bend over."

She bent over, and all the color rushed to her face and set it on fire. She waited. The first blow stung her bottom, and she winced. The next one hurt even more.

"Sadie, I have told you over and over not to be the momma or the papa of this family. You did it once too often."

Sadie sniffed back a sob. She wasn't ready for the next spank, and it almost knocked her over.

"You will never call your sister a liar again." Momma spanked her one more time. "And you will not lie!"

Sadie stood with her hands at her sides, even though she wanted to rub her bottom to ease the pain. She stared at her dirty feet. She wanted to scream at Helen and shake the truth from her, but she knew Momma wouldn't allow it.

"Sadie, you're much too old to be spanked, but that's what I had to do to make you know how terrible your conduct was. I want you to apologize to Helen right now."

Helen shrank against Opal.

Sadie breathed deeply. Why should she apologize when she was right?

"Sadie," said Momma.

"I'm sorry for spanking you, Helen."

"Continue," said Momma.

Sadie looked right at Helen and saw the pain in her eyes. "I'm sorry for calling you a liar."

Helen buried her face in Opal's dress.

"What do you say, Helen?" said Momma.

Helen slowly lifted her head. "I forgive you, Sadie."

Sadie pressed her lips together in one straight, tight line.

"It's too late in the day to rewash the clothes." Momma turned away. "You children go about your work. All is back to normal now. When the clothes are dry, we'll shake them good. If the dirt doesn't come off, we'll wash them again tomorrow."

Sadie ran to the garden and began to hoe weeds that weren't even there. Sand flew, and finally she stopped before she hoed up the seeds that would make their winter food.

When she finished, she looked for Helen and finally found her playing all alone under Momma's tree. Sadie sat down and Helen scooted back, looking frightened.

"Why did you lie?" asked Sadie in a low, tight voice.

Helen, seeing no one around, whispered, "If you can, so can I."

Sadie gasped and felt weak all over. She'd never thought about her bad actions affecting anyone else. How wrong she'd been!

"I'm tired of being a good little girl all the time. I want to do bad things like you do."

Sadie hung her head.

"What's wrong, Sadie?"

"I don't want you to be a bad girl, Helen. It'll make you feel sad and lonely and . . . awful!"

Helen pulled her knees to her chin and pulled her dress down to her ankles. "I don't feel sad or lonely or awful."

"How do you feel?"

"Glad for not gettin' another spankin'."

"What about makin' a mess on the clothes?"

"It was an accident. I didn't think about them bein' there, and when I ran after Toady I stepped all over them. But I'll help wash them again."

"You know Momma always says a lie will eat you up."

Helen nodded. "I thought about that, but when it didn't eat you up, I didn't figure it'd eat me up. I'm about as tough as you."

Tears slowly slipped down Sadie's cheek, and she brushed them away and wiped the back of her hand across her nose.

"Why're you cryin', Sadie?"

"I don't want you to be a bad girl, Helen. I don't want to be a bad girl either. But it's too late for me. It isn't for you." Sadie took Helen's small hand in hers. "Go tell Momma the truth. She won't spank you. She never spanks someone for telling the truth."

Helen thought about it for a long time and finally she shook her head. "No. It's too late for me too."

"Oh, Helen."

"Don't cry, Sadie. You and me will be bad girls together."

A laugh burst from Sadie and she grabbed Helen and hugged her hard, laughing and crying at the same time.

13

Tanner

Sadie chewed a piece of prairie chicken and forced herself to swallow it. She glanced at Helen and saw that she was having just as much trouble eating Momma's good supper. Since Monday, they'd both picked at their food and had had a hard time joining in with the others, even when York played his guitar so they could sing together.

One day York strummed a few chords and then said, "Someday we won't need to have the covered wagon set up for a house for you kids. We'll have a house where we can sit on chairs and sing together and talk together. We'll come out and watch the stars and the moon and sing when we want, but we'll have a house. I promise you that. I promise you, Bess."

"Oh, York," said Momma with tears in her voice.

York struck a happy chord and sang "Old Dan Tucker," and Momma's pretty voice joined with York's. Sadie looked away to hide her tears.

Helen slipped her hand in Sadie's and whispered in her ear, "Don't cry. I love you even if you're bad. And so does Jesus. I asked Momma and she said so. She said Jesus doesn't like bad things that people do, but He loves the people."

Sadie couldn't speak without sobbing aloud. She wanted to tell Helen to go back to being the good girl she'd been, and that more than anything she wanted to do the same. She squeezed Helen's hand and forced herself to join in. Somehow she had to find a way to help Helen.

The next morning, just after chores, Sadie with Tanner beside her stood back from the wagon as it pulled out of the yard with Momma sitting beside York on the seat and Web, Helen, and Opal in the back. Riley was with the cattle. Sadie had said she wanted to stay home from town and York had said, "I reckon it's safe enough. I scouted around the past two days and never saw hide nor hair of Ty Bailer. I heard he left for Montana. Besides, Riley will be back quicker than you can say jackrabbit."

So Momma had agreed to let her stay. Helen had asked if she wanted her to stay with her, but Sadie said no and Helen had been glad. She'd skipped to the wagon, dressed in the blue gingham that Momma had made from Opal's old dress. She waved until they were out of sight.

Sadie sighed loud and long. "It's just you and me, Tanner. I'm glad you're feeling well enough to walk around some."

Tanner waved his flag of a tail and whined as if

he understood every word she said. His brown coat
shone, and his dark eyes were alert.

"It's gonna be a while before you can run a rabbit, but with me takin' care of you, you'll do it yet.
Won't you, boy?"

Tanner barked a short bark that she took for a
yes.

She walked slowly toward the soddy, her hand
resting lightly on Tanner's head. She'd promised
Momma she'd stuff a new mattress tick with grasses
that they'd cut and dried. Usually Momma used hay,
but York had said good wild hay smelled sweeter and
felt better than hay you'd plant yourself.

In the soddy she touched York's Bible and
thought about the verses on God's blessings he'd read
to them after they'd eaten breakfast.

Once God's blessings had belonged to her, but
not since she had pulled away from Him. She didn't
deserve His blessings at all. She deserved to burn in
Hell forever and ever, the way the preacher had said
on his last visit before Pa had died. Momma had said
that the preacher should've explained clearer that
people who didn't accept Jesus as personal Savior
would burn in Hell, not everyone who did something
wrong.

"We all do wrong things from time to time,"
Momma had said to Pa when she thought everyone
else was asleep, but Sadie had been awake and listening. She was afraid she'd burn in Hell forever and
ever because she'd wanted Emma to lose the spelling
bee so she could win. Sadie had known how bad she'd
been to think that, but she had thought it. She didn't
want to burn in Hell, so she'd listened carefully to
what Momma was saying. "We all do wrong things,

but Jesus forgives us when we ask and He helps us to do better."

"Preacher Donnelson said we're all sinners headed for Hellfire."

"But the Bible talks about forgiveness, about God being love, about everlasting life for the believer."

Sadie had fallen asleep before she'd heard Pa's final answer. She touched York's Bible and wished she hadn't. She deserved to burn forever in Hell for causing Pa's death, but Helen didn't deserve to burn for the lie Sadie herself had made her tell.

"Oh, Helen, don't let me make you suffer."

Tanner whined and looked at her.

"It's all right, Tanner. I'm talking to myself." She hugged his neck and then walked to the mattress tick that they'd already emptied, and reached for the dried grasses that Riley had brought in and piled beside the bed.

Tanner sniffed at the stove that was almost cold and at the chairs and the table. Then he laid down in the doorway in the warm sun. Above the doorway hung the rifle that had belonged to Pa. Riley had taught her and Opal and Web how to use it. It was too heavy for Helen.

After what seemed a long time to Sadie, she finished stuffing the mattress. Carefully she whip-stitched it closed with tiny stitches that wouldn't break easily. The only sounds inside the house were Momma's mantle clock and the little noises Tanner made as he slept. The outdoor noises were soaked up by the thick walls of sod.

Suddenly Tanner lifted his head, his pointed ears even more pointed. He stood and growled deep in his chest.

The hair on the back of Sadie's neck stood on end. She remembered that Racer had growled that way to let them know of nearby danger.

What danger did Tanner smell or feel?

Sadie inched toward the door and stood on a chair to lift down the loaded rifle.

Tanner whined and settled back down, and she breathed easier. York had told Riley to come back just as soon as he'd checked the windmill. Maybe Tanner had smelled Riley, but had given a warning growl.

She gripped the rifle tighter. "I'll keep the rifle down, just in case."

In case of Ty Bailer?

She pushed the ugly thought aside. York had said he was long gone.

But she carried the rifle with her as she walked out to move Bossie and take her water. She took it with her to check the hen that they'd named Cluck. The crate was open so Cluck could scratch for food when she wanted. Most of the time she sat on her eggs and scolded if anyone came close, or pecked if anyone tried to touch her.

Sadie watered Momma's tree and touched a leaf and stroked the trunk. "You're a good tree. Someday you'll be big and tall and shade the house for the family. But I won't be here." Her voice broke, and she couldn't continue.

She gazed out across the prairie hoping to sight Riley. Grasses waved in the wind. Birds flew and sang. But there was no sign of Riley.

Tanner growled, and Sadie's heart stood still. She looked at the rifle that she'd left beside the well when she'd filled a bucket for Momma's tree.

"We meet again, prairie chicken."

She turned slowly to find Ty Bailer at the corner of the house. His salt-and-pepper beard covered the front of his shirt. His pants were patched and faded. She tried to speak, but her voice was gone.

Rifle in hand at his side, he walked toward her. She noticed his boots were dusty, as if he'd been walking a while. He'd probably left his mule out of sight behind a hill and walked to the yard. "Cat got yer tongue?"

"I thought . . . we thought you were . . . gone."

He stopped about five feet from her. "I got me a score to settle. Tyler Bailer never walks away from an unsettled score."

Tanner growled again, and Sadie put her hand on the bristling hair on his neck.

"Move away from the pup."

"No."

"I shoot the pup first and then take you out for the buzzards to eat." He lifted his rifle.

Sadie leaped forward and knocked the rifle up just as the shot fired. Her ears rang.

Ty Bailer swung the rifle down, but before he could chamber another round a blur of fur passed Sadie and struck Ty Bailer, knocking him to the ground. The rifle fell away from him, and without thought Sadie grabbed it and aimed it at the man and dog writhing on the ground.

"Oh, Tanner," she whispered. She knew how weak he was and how strong Ty Bailer was.

Tanner held Bailer by the wrist and shook him, growling and snarling. Bailer slugged Tanner over and over with his free fist, but Tanner held on, shaking the wrist hard enough to jerk Bailer around. The old man lifted his feet and tried to kick Tanner, but

130

couldn't. Dust flew, and yelling and snarling filled the air.

Sadie stepped closer and shouted, "Don't hit Tanner again."

"Call off yer dog!"

"Stop hittin' him!"

"I'm bleedin'."

"Stop hittin' him!"

"Call it off now!"

"Stop hittin' him and I will."

"I stopped. I stopped!"

She waited until he actually stopped and then she shouted, "Tanner! Come here, boy!"

Tanner snarled and shook Bailer's arm harder.

"You mangy mutt!" Bailer pulled back his free arm and slammed his fist against Tanner's head near his eye. Tanner yelped and fell back. Bailer grabbed for the knife at his thigh, but Tanner lunged against him and sent him falling back on the ground. Bailer caught Tanner by the throat and flung him hard to the ground.

Tanner yelped and lay still.

Sadie trembled, and the rifle shook in her hands. Tanner had saved her life, and she had to save his.

Bailer pulled his knife, and the blade flashed in the sunlight. Sadie shot, spitting up sand just inches from Bailer's foot.

"Drop that knife," she said in a voice that sounded more like Momma's than hers.

He watched her through narrowed slits of eyes.

"Drop it!"

Tanner lifted his head and pushed himself unsteadily to his feet. He growled at Bailer, and the old man dropped the knife.

"Good boy, Tanner. Come here."

Tanner half-walked, half-dragged himself to her, stood beside her, and faced Ty with her.

Pounding hoofbeats filled the air, and seconds later Riley landed with a thud beside her, his feet spread, a rifle in his hands, aimed right at the old man. "Ty Bailer?"

"Yes."

"Good work, Sadie."

"I'm glad you came."

"I heard the shots. Keep your sights on him, and I'll get my rope and tie him so tight he'll never get away."

"What're you kids doin' to me? I didn't mean no harm."

Tanner growled.

Sadie watched as Riley looped the rope around Bailer's arms and chest and then down to his ankles. Bailer cursed and threatened and pleaded.

Riley stepped back and hooked his thumbs in his belt. "No more talk, Mr. Bailer."

"Let me go and I'll never bother ya again," he said.

Riley turned to Sadie. "We'll save him for York."

She nodded and handed the rifle to Riley, then dropped to her knees beside Tanner. "Good dog. I love you, Tanner."

14
The Storm

York leaned against the wagon and looked up at Sadie on the seat. "Sadie Rose, you are a brave girl."

She flushed with pride at York's words. "Tanner and Riley helped too."

"That's the truth, but you stood up to Ty and didn't back down." York pushed back his hat. "Thanks to Joshua Cass, Ty Bailer is behind bars where he can't hurt you again."

"I'm glad."

As York turned to check a bawling calf, Sadie looked up at the slowly turning windmill and listened to the water running into the big tank. Cattle milled around the tank, some drinking, some grazing, and they all carried York's brand on their flanks, a big Ⓨ. A calf ran and kicked up its heels.

Sadie smiled slightly. She was glad Riley had gone hunting with Levi and that York had brought her to help him. She'd had a chance to talk with Levi when he'd first ridden up on his black mare, smiling and excited about hunting.

"Ty Bailer won't bother you ever again, Sadie," he'd said while he waited for Riley to saddle Bay.

"And Tanner's safe." Sadie hugged Tanner and then smiled at Levi. He had smiled back, and she'd known they were special friends no matter what his relationship with Opal became.

Suddenly a gust of cold wind sent the windmill blades spinning fast. Sadie jumped and shivered, even with her coat on.

York looked up to see gray clouds skidding across the gray sky. "A storm's brewin'. I'd best get you home, Sadie Rose."

Dick and Jane pranced and snorted, and Sadie held tighter to the reins while York shut the windmill off.

Dick snorted again and Jane reared, then they lunged forward, jerking the reins from Sadie's hands. She bounced on the seat and almost bounced over the front of the wagon. She grabbed the seat with one hand, reached for the reins with the other, and pressed her wide-spread feet against the wagon floor for balance.

"Whoa!" she shouted.

"Dick! Jane!" York yelled and whistled and ran after the wagon as it lurched and bounced across the prairie.

The team raced around a hill, and the wagon bucked harder. Sadie tipped back, and her feet shot into the air. She landed in the wagon bed with a thud. She tried to get up, but was tossed back down. She turned on her stomach and worked her way to the seat, wrapped her arms around it, and inched her way up to get the reins. They were gone—draped over the tongue, dragging the ground.

"I can't get them," she whispered hoarsely.

Her feet flew up, and she almost lost her grip on the seat. This time she carefully made her way to the *back* of the wagon, then sat in a corner, her knees to her chin. She'd have to wait until Dick and Jane stopped before she could get the reins.

Cold rain began to lash against her. Her sunbonnet drooped against her head, and her clothes clung to her slight body. She shivered. Suddenly the rain turned to giant white flakes that swirled in the air and filled it until she could barely see Dick and Jane.

Sadie whimpered and pulled tighter into herself. Was a blizzard finally going to kill her to get even with her for Pa?

Her mind flashed to York. Would York die too?

"Please, God, please, God, don't let him die. Keep him safe. Keep me safe." The words were tiny sounds in the thundering of the hooves and the creak of the wagon.

Finally Dick and Jane slowed to a walk and then stopped altogether with their heads down. Steam streamed from their soft noses and mixed with the huge white flakes. The silence pressed against Sadie and frightened her. Slowly she eased herself over the wagon and climbed down the wheel. She didn't want to make any sudden movement that would send Dick and Jane off again.

At the front of the wagon she spoke to them gently and picked up the reins, wrapping them securely on the wagon. She walked around the team, talking softly. Dick snorted, and Jane nickered.

"We have to go back for York. You're both going to be good and not run away again. We have to get York before he freezes."

Shivering she climbed up on the wagon seat, uncurled the reins, and held them firmly and slapped them against Dick and Jane. They stepped forward in their best manner.

The white swirls of snow stopped as quickly as they had started, and rain fell in huge drops. Sadie watched snow disappear from the grasses and the wagon and her. Water soaked through her shoes, turning her feet icy cold.

She looked all around to find her bearings. Dick shook the harness, and Sadie gripped the reins tighter, but not so tight that the team stopped.

York had said while they were driving out to the cattle, "You can know where you're at by the hills, Sadie Rose."

She'd looked around, but all the hills seemed the same.

"See that pointed hill between the two small hills?"

"Yes."

"I named that hill Point." He grinned at her. "I name the hills. The one over there I call Jackrabbit Hill because that's where I shot my first jackrabbit after I claimed this land. And that one is Ball. It's a short hill, but big around. Those hills never change no matter the season. I watch the hills, and I know where I'm at."

She'd smiled in amazement when she saw that the hills weren't all just alike, and she'd memorized the shapes and the names he told her as they rode to the pasture.

She blinked the rain from her eyes now and shook her head and shivered.

As the team trotted along, Sadie looked around for a familiar hill. Finally she spotted Point, and she knew she wasn't far from the homestead. Dick and Jane had been on their way home. She turned them. She would not go back until she had York in the wagon with her.

She called to the team and urged them to go faster. The rain ceased and the sun popped out, turning the sky brilliant blue. Once she had to stop and look around again, but she saw Ball and she knew she wasn't lost.

"Sadie Rose!"

Her name floated to her, and she looked around and found York walking toward her. He was soaked and looked cold. She waved, and he waved back.

"Get up, Dick, Jane!"

When she reached York, she stopped Dick and Jane and burst into tears.

York leaped into the wagon, took the reins, and pulled her close in his wet arms.

She sobbed against him as the wagon rolled slowly along. Finally she moved away from him, but he wouldn't let her go far. Her cheeks flamed, and she couldn't look at him. "I know I'm too big to cry."

He touched her cheek with the tip of his finger. "Suppose you tell me what caused the tears."

"I didn't want you to die . . . too."

"Too?"

"Like Pa did. In a blizzard." Her voice rose. "Because of me."

"You weren't to blame."

"But I was!" She kept her eyes on the tips of his

wet boots. "He went lookin' for me, and he died, and all the time I was safe and snug at Emma's."

He rubbed her hand. "Does your momma know you blame yourself?"

She lifted her head. "Momma and the others pretend they don't remember, but I know they do. I know they really do hate me, but they pretend to love me."

"Oh, little Sadie Rose." He stroked her wet hair. "You've been carryin' around a big burden for such little shoulders. It's time you dropped it off."

"No."

"You know about forgivin' others, Sadie Rose, but it's time you learned about forgivin' yourself."

"No!"

"You can't carry guilt around forever. It's bad on you and on your family around you."

She thought of Helen and her lie, and she knew York was right.

"Nothing you do will change the past. Your pa is dead, if it be your fault or not."

"I deserve to burn in Hell forever and ever!" Oh, but she didn't want to!

"But you won't, because you gave yourself to Jesus. He suffered and He died so that you wouldn't have to. He rose again to give you eternal life in Heaven. When you accept what He's done for you, then you won't go to Hell when you die."

"But I deserve to!"

"We all deserve to, Sadie Rose. No one sin is greater than any other. You know that. But Jesus said we don't have to pay for our sins because He already did. He doesn't want you to carry around guilt over your pa. Jesus wants you to forgive yourself and go on living for Him."

Sadie sniffed and leaned against York. "I have been so bad! I lied and I disobeyed Momma and I argued with Helen and Web and Opal. And I spied on Opal and Levi!"

York held her close again as Dick and Jane plodded along like a pair of workhorses. "Ask Jesus to forgive you and He will. And He'll help you forgive yourself."

Hope rose in Sadie.

"Why don't you pray now. Never wait until tomorrow if you can settle it today." York bowed his head over Sadie's.

Sadie bit her lip and then whispered, "Jesus, I'm sorry for my lies and for disobeying and for fighting and for spying on Opal. Make my heart clean and help me to . . . to forgive myself for making Pa . . . die in the blizzard. I'm sorry I was safe and snug in Emma's house. I'm sorry for making Pa go out in the blizzard after me. I don't want to feel guilty any longer, and I don't want to burn in Hell forever and ever." Every word seemed to send a shaft of light into her heart until suddenly she felt as if she glowed inside as bright as the sun was shining after the storm.

York said, "Father God, thank You for giving all Your blessings to my precious Sadie Rose."

Sadie wrapped her arms around York's neck and hugged him so hard she almost knocked his hat off.

Several minutes later at their place, Sadie jumped from the wagon and helped York unhitch Dick and Jane. She led Jane into the barn and York led Dick.

Just as Sadie finished forking hay for Jane, she heard little peep-peeping sounds. She looked in the crate to find the eggs cracked open and tiny balls of yellow fluff peeping at the top of their lungs.

"I'll be switched," said York, lifting a ball into his hand. "You're a pretty little thing." He turned to Sadie and laughed. "This cowboy never touched a baby chick before."

Sadie rubbed one against her cheek and then put it back.

Cluck half-flew, half-ran into the barn, clucking angrily.

"We're not hurting your babies," said York. He set the chick back down. Carefully he turned the crate on its side, fixed the nest, and the chicks ran out to Cluck. He caught Sadie's hand. "Let's go to the house. We have a lot to tell your momma."

She ran to the house with York taking long strides behind her. She burst through the door. "I'm home, Momma!" In her heart she knew she was home to stay and would no longer have to leave to be by Pa's empty body.

With York right behind her, she stopped short just inside the room. Momma, Web, and Opal stood around Helen, who was crying into her hands. "What's wrong?"

Helen ran to Sadie. "I couldn't be a bad girl any longer. It hurt too much. So I told."

Sadie hugged her close. "Good for you. I'll tell too."

York slipped his arm around her and she said, "I have something to say if it's all right with you, Momma."

Momma bit her lip and nodded.

In a firm voice that shook only a little when she looked at Opal, Sadie told them everything. When she finished, Momma opened her arms and Sadie walked into them. The others crowded around, talking all at the same time.

After a long time Sadie said, "And I have a great surprise."

"What?" asked Helen and Web.

"Cluck's chicks hatched. I counted twelve of them."